MW01274355

# The Search for Harry C

## Mort Altshuler &

## Irv Susson

| Library of Congress Number: | | 00-193515 |
|---|---|---|
| ISBN #: | Softcover | 0-7388-4553-1 |

This is a work of fiction. Names, characters, places and incidents
either are the product of the author's imagination or are used
fictitiously, and any resemblance to any actual persons, living or
dead, events, or locales is entirely coincidental.

This book was printed in the United States of America.

**To order additional copies of this book, contact:**
Xlibris Corporation
1-888-7-XLIBRIS
www.Xlibris.com
Orders@Xlibris.com

*for Katherine and Barbara*

# Author's Note

*Our profound thanks to Amy, Gary and Nate Lebo, Joseph Altshuler, Pam, Gregory, Jaclyn and Brett Hollander for their support during the writing of this book.*

*M.A. & I. S.*

# PREFACE

The first atomic bomb in history was detonated at a site called Trinity, near Alamogordo, New Mexico.

*AUGUST 6, 1945*

The Enola Gay, a Boeing B-29, dropped an atom bomb named "Little Boy" on Hiroshima, Japan, at 8:15 in the morning.

*APRIL 18, 1953: NEVADA PROVING GROUND*

Harry Connors vanished today, the day that a 23-kiloton Atomic Bomb was detonated atop a 300-foot tower in Area 2, of the Nevada Test Site.

# PART 1

# THE DISAPPEARANCE

MARCH 15, 1953: MOSCOW, USSR

Anatoly Dusplatov, a ranking member of the KGB, was Director, Special Tasks, for all of Europe and North America. This division of the KGB controlled all acts of espionage and assassination. He sat behind his paneled desk reading the latest cables, received during the last 24 hours. One in particular held his interest. His creased forehead indicated his concentration on the communication from the American with the code name, 'Paris'. Dusplatov reached for the intercom on his phone, lifted the receiver and spoke quietly but with great authority.

"Send Pavel in."

The door opened quickly and Pavel Sanofsky entered and stood in front of the desk. This slight man of medium stature was the head of the Scientific Section of the Foreign Directorate who reported directly to Dusplatov. He was handed the cable that so interested his superior.

"Pavel, explain to me the meaning of this message, but please don't bake it in a crust of scientific dribble."

Sanofsky, still standing, read the document quickly. His eyes closed momentarily as if to allow the information to rearrange itself in a more meaningful context.

"Comrade Director, if this information is correct, then the recent American Atomic bomb tests, have yielded a far greater residue of radioactivity then was anticipated. It is what the Americans call 'dirty'. I do not have the wind patterns at hand, but if they are in line with the prevailing wind patterns previously recorded during the past, then a full third of the American continent could have been affected by radiation fallout."

"And the consequences of this fallout?"

"Even without further data, Comrade, I can tell you that the level of fallout will produce some long-term health problems for the population in that area."

"What is your immediate reaction to this turn of events?"

"Perhaps if our contacts in America could somehow make this public knowledge, there would be a public outcry condemning their government for lacking concern for their citizens. This would, surely, slow their testing program and would give us needed time to catch up and even surpass them."

"Hmm, no doubt, no doubt. No, Pavel, let's not spill what our friends call the beans. I will take a bit of time to consider this."

*MARCH 17, 1953: INDIAN SPRINGS AFB, NEVADA*

Lt. Bert Foley (USNR) was getting into his jeep in front of the small mess hall, his passenger, Lt. Comdr. "Puffy" Spearson (USN), had to be at the drone control van in twenty minutes and he seemed to be in a particularly pissy mood. It was a bit after 2:30 AM and Bert had been looking forward to the start of this day. Recently, he looked forward to every day, for he had spent all of his childhood playing and dreaming of aircraft. Now the Navy paid him a decent wage to play with a Douglas AD Skyraider. Developed after WWII, it was known to be extremely durable and capable of carrying large loads. Bert marveled that the six-ton craft could carry six tons. It was for this reason and the fact that the Skyraider could easily sustain itself at almost seven-mile altitude, that the

Navy had transformed this beauty into a laboratory of sorts and into a drone. The craft could be flown manually, controlled from the ground or from a chase plane. Puffy's job was to ground-control this pilot-less aircraft, and Bert's job was to control from the chase plane.

## MARCH 17, 1953 LAS VEGAS, NEVADA

Harry Connors wife, Sarah, was right out of the old song, 'five foot two, eyes of blue'. Her blond hair was short, pleasant to look at and she bounced a little when she walked. Most people found her to be energetic, honest and a great friend. Sarah put the dishes and coffee cups in the sink and headed for the shower. It was one of those home made things with an old claw-footed tub and curtains around it. She always had trouble finding the opening. No never-mind, however, as long as Harry kept the 'scuzz' off the inner shower curtain. Under the water, she ruminated about what she had learned about her new town since their recent arrival. Always under the impression that a movie she saw told the true tale, it wasn't the gambling interests that founded the town. She had gone to the library in town and had read that in 1855 Brigham Young had sent some young Mormons to the area to build a fort and convert the locals and teach them farming. A couple of years later, the settlement and the project were abandoned. The Piutes had made a mess of the provisions, ruined the crops and let all the livestock go. The Mormons had tried their luck in mining, but gave up, for the lead they were mining was difficult to work and cast. About a decade later, it was found that the "lead" was really silver ore! Around the turn of the century the San Pedro, Los Angeles & Salt Lake Railroad Company purchased the area of the original townsite and Las Vegas was legally created in 1905. Sarah figured as she toweled herself dry, that in 48 years the town had grown to about 25,000 and it attracted 7 million tourists a year. She was pleased about the tourists, for she had no trouble finding a job when she got here.

Sarah, now dressed in her waitress uniform, headed down the porch steps with some clothes for the cleaner to be dropped off on her way to the early shift. She headed toward Fremont Street, stopped at Greenstein's cleaners, then around the corner into the parking lot and the back door of the El Cortez Hotel. She really liked the job and the people in the Buccaneer Bar, but she did not particularly enjoy it when many of the regulars coming in would ask, "where's your buccaneers?" and all the help had to respond, "Under my buccan hat!" She had had an offer from Benny Binion's Horseshoe Saloon at Second, but the pay and the shifts were better at the Cortez. Her mind drifted to thoughts of Harry and her concern for his safety during the atomic detonations.

*MARCH 17, 1953: INDIAN SPRINGS AFB,*

*NEVADA—SHOT "ANNIE", 4:35AM*

LTJG B.K. Kelly, call sign "ABLE," climbed into the cockpit of the Skyraider drone and started his engine as Chief Petty Officer Dutch Mitchell stood by with the fire extinguisher. He pressed his microphone button and called LCdr. Puffy Spearson, call sign "FOX," seated at his console in the operations van.

"FOX, I'm ready to check out the bird."

Spearson initiated a series of checks designed to verify the reliability of his control of the drone's flight systems and instrumentation. He carefully noted the aircraft response on his own duplicate set of the aircraft's instruments. Satisfied, he called Kelly.

"ABLE, my check is complete, you can taxi in position."

Kelly taxied the drone away from the hangar onto the taxi strip that would lead him to the runway. It was still an hour before sunup, but he knew that, shortly, the whole sky would be ablaze from the 16-kiloton detonation scheduled that morning. As he taxied toward the runway, he saw CHARLIE ONE and TWO, the chase planes, taking off side by side, carrier style. CHARLIE ONE, a Grumman F8F Bearcat piloted by Lt. Bert Foley, had the capability of controlling the drone and would do so for its return leg of the hop. CHARLIE TWO, a Douglas F4D Skyray piloted by Lt. Byron Peterson, was armed, and in the event of an errant drone, his mission was to "splash" it. Kelly reached the end of the runway and lined up the aircraft for takeoff. He climbed out of the aircraft after Spearson assured him he had control. Parked alongside of the drone with their engines running, were a jeep and a van. They had followed Kelly from the hangar. Kelly climbed into the jeep for his trip back to the hangar. As the jeep left, the van driven by Dutch Mitchell took its place alongside of the drone. Mitchell opened the rear door of the van and proceeded to pull out a dummy dressed in a flight suit, which he placed in the pilot's seat. Fearful that there would be a public outcry about people's safety with pilot-less aircraft flying around, the Navy decided to put a dummy pilot in the aircraft. Even that didn't work out too well all the time, for there had been a recent incident where a drone had crashed and a good Samaritan bystander had tried vainly to save the pilot, not realizing it was a dummy.

After completing his tasks which included plugging in the instrumentation package that Harry Connors and Dick Tishman had designed for the dummy, Mitchell called Spearson from the radio in his van and reported that the drone was ready for takeoff. Spearson then called the chase plane for a systems check. After CHARLIE ONE had checked out his system, Spearson took back control. He looked at the drone sitting on the runway and could see that, further down, numerous fire trucks with their rotating lights flashing were on stand-by in the event of an emergency. Puffy hit his microphone button and spoke.

6-ALTS

"Indian Springs, NAVY 225 ready to roll."

"NAVY 225 you're cleared for takeoff at your discretion, all other traffic on hold until you're airborne."

Spearson sat at his console in the telemetering van. In front of him was essentially, a duplicate set of aircraft controls and instrumentation. On his left was a radar plot, which would pinpoint the drone's position continuously. This radar plot overlaid a map of the test area on which was drawn a prescribed flight path that he would follow.

Connors and Tishman sat at their consoles at the other end of the van. Mitchell returned from the flight line and took his place at one of the consoles. He and his men were responsible for recording all data and communications during the operation.

After checking with CHARLIE ONE and TWO, Spearson initiated the sequence that would get the drone airborne.

The Skyraider drone rose gracefully into the air and started its climb toward its designated altitude of 5000 feet, with the chase planes flying in loose formation. In addition to their own radio channel, all personnel of the ground and in the air were monitoring the countdown using split headphones. At H-hour minus two minutes, Puffy turned the drone on its final heading of 280 degrees to put it in the proper position at detonation. Foley and Peterson, flying the chase planes, lowered their blast shields over their eyes. At H-hour, blinding white light, obliterating their vision totally, illuminated both their cockpits. Four and a half seconds later, both their aircraft were buffeted and they struggled to maintain control. They were warned about the pressure wave that had just hit them but were surprised at its intensity.

"CHARLIE, FOX—You guys OK?"

"I think so, FOX—that was one big kick in the ass."

"Anyone have a visual on the bird?"

"Negative, FOX—we're still trying to get oriented, give me some smoke."

Spearson turned on a smoke generator in the drone to facilitate a visual sighting.

"Roger that CHARLIE—I show the bird at your 11 o'clock position and smoke is on."

"FOX—CHARLIE TWO—I have a tally-ho dead ahead."

"FOX—CHARLIE ONE—closing on the bird and ready for control."

"CHARLIE ONE, this is FOX—take control."

"Roger, I have control."

Foley put the drone in a shallow right turn and headed back to Indian Springs. As he made his final approach while flying wing on the drone, he called the tower with his usual, "Indian Springs, I have a full house, three gear and two flaps" and was told he was cleared to land. The drone touched down softly on the runway, and he brought it to a safe stop. The drone was surrounded immediately by the ground crew who proceeded to wash it down with heavy sprays of water from a pumper truck to wash off any radiation that remained.

### APRIL 1, 1953: MOSCOW, USSR

In a familiar role, Pavel Sanofsky stood in front of the desk of his superior and awaited his instructions. Director Dusplatov stood behind his desk staring intently at Sanofsky.

"Pavel, I've have come up with a plan for our friends in Nevada. It is imperative that we keep the high radiation information quiet, and let them destroy themselves. Send the following cable at once, 'Order the Trojan Prince to bring the Queen of Sparta home, the family needs her.' Listen carefully and put these orders into immediate action!"

*APRIL 17, 1953, LAS VEGAS, NEVADA:*

Sarah Conners brushed toast crumbs off the front of Harry's sweater as he leaned to kiss her goodbye. Today was the day for the next scheduled detonation, and she hoped it would be as successful as the first. The last words that she heard, as she swallowed the last of her coffee was, "See you tomorrow night". Harry, a head and a half taller at 6'1", was a basketball player type, sort of a controlled, gangly—gaited young man with an almost handsome and pleasant face. He smiled a lot, but rarely showed his teeth when he did. Sarah liked the faint, small crescent-shaped scar on his left cheek; the only thing left of a fight with another 9 year-old. Harry had told her long ago that it had been his only fight in his whole life and he was trying to stop the other kid from making fun of one of their classmates. Smiling, he glanced at the clock near the kitchen door, noted the 6:45 AM time, waved and stepped out on their second floor porch. Actually, it was their only porch and only entrance; up a flight of solid wooden steps to their temporary, rented second floor apartment. The rent was reasonable, the place was pleasant and it was four streets off of Fremont Street, well away from the noise and glitter and that damn big neon cowboy at the Pioneer. Harry didn't mind the 50-minute drive each way to Desert Rock or the airbase at Indian Springs. He could have had quarters at the base, but there were no facilities for families. Sarah wanted to be close and Harry had always said he needed it that way. Anyway, the 60 miles into the wastelands that was Desert Rock was flat, fast, mostly straight and it gave Harry time to get the cotton out of his head, think about the day ahead and to listen to the good western radio station. They played many of his favorites often, like Ernest Tubbs, and that was OK with him. Harry would shout over the motor noise all the words to "Everybody's Lonely For Somebody Else, But Nobody's Lonely For Me" while speeding across the desert with the sun about three clicks above dawn, warming the nape of his neck through the back window of his coupe. He pulled into the dirt parking area at Camp Desert Rock at 7:55 am. Some "camp", he mused, it was only a community of large 8-man tents put up by the Army for the troops participating in the activities at the Nevada test site of the Atomic Energy Commission. There were a few more permanent buildings like the mess hall and the administrative and research house. All made of wood, sort of brownish like the tents, the desert, the brush, the military garb, Yuck!—not a bit of color and looking a lot like a badly done sepia print. The cars had some color if you looked toward the parking area and he and other civilians, at least, were able to wear some brightly shaded shirts, usually with khakis. Loafers were "big", and Harry trotted his pair over to the mess hall where a pot of coffee always puffed and steamed ready to burn your tongue. Harry, after the drive through the desert, wished he had stopped for some Danish at 'Foxy's' on his way out of town, to have with his Java. At 24, he felt that he was still growing and needed it.

### APRIL 17, 1953: DESERT ROCK, NEVADA

By 8:15 AM Harry, with his feet on his small, badly scuffed Army desk, reviewed his important files. All the last-minute actions for the final 18 hours before detonation "zero-hour" had to be A-one perfect.

Harry and his five-man crew had positioned all the radiation detection devices around the tower in ever-increasing concentric circles. Some instruments were placed in various protective jury rigs. These placements employed many different materials in the form of covers, shields and the like to determine their future use as heat and radiation protective devices. A few detection units were buried in small holes and others were placed inside small concrete bunkers of various thicknesses.

Assistance and consultation were also offered to a small U.S. Navy Neurologic Research team. The team leader and Harry determined where and how the placement of about fifty live animals was to be accomplished. This was done in a small pie-shaped section, with its point at ground zero and emanating outward about 3000 yards. Harry, always able to get things done efficiently, quickly and economically, suggested that the Navy save their time and money. He had the Navy team move the mostly chickens, rabbits, pigs and a few goats in with all his detection devices, for all the protection array was already in place. Harry was easy on them.

"Hey, guys, the rent for your animals in our little quarters out there will be cheap."

"Whaddaya mean, cheap?"

"Simple, you get to save all your time and we give you all the radiation data first-hand and all you got to do is two things."

"Oh, yeah! Here it comes——"

"No, really, it's simple. You buy me beer in the 'gedunk' for the week you're here and you get to clean up all the chicken shit off my nice equipment after that blast. How's that?"

"As the team honcho, I agree, with pleasure 'cause I won't be among the cleanup crew!"

Harry spent the bulk of the day with his team checking out all the equipment and the map coordinates relative to the correct placement of each. This had been the third time this had been done in the last three days, but it was crucial. This occupied so much time that Harry realized that he was hungry as hell, for they hadn't stopped for lunch. They had mucho water with them, but no food. About midnight, the crew and Harry went to the mess hall, which was always open, 24 hours a day, for the heavy workweek before a detonation.

*APRIL 18, 1953: DESERT ROCK, NEVADA*

Shortly after midnight Harry gulped the last of his root beer soda from the mess hall and unlocked his office door and entered what the Army, facetiously, called an office. It was a 5' by 7' cubbyhole. The door was made of ¾" plywood so secure that he could have kicked it open. But you didn't even have to do that. His laminated ID card poked into the door-jamb next to the doorknob would unlatch the door faster than breaking it down. He always left it unlocked, but the security Military Police types would report it and then he would have to spend precious time sitting in front of the camp command-ing officer listening to a lecture about security. It had become easier to just lock the damn thing. It was about 12:45 AM and a little red alert light on his phone was blinking. He sat at the desk and pressed the number for the camp office. A corporal, on duty at the Master at Arms office, responded.

"Mr. Connors, a Mr. Tishman at Indian Springs Air Force Base down the road, called and he said you were to get him, even if you have to send a runner, as soon as you can."

"Thanks, can you get the base and contact him for me? I'll hold on."

"Sure, sir, wait one."

"Harry, that you?"

"Of course, you schmuck, are you, maybe, expecting Paulette Goddard?"

"Listen, no crap, I got a call from the flight-line and they report some malfunction of the reception modules on the drone and one on the dummy. They were going through their final checklist and came up with garbled shit. Can you get here an hour ago?"

"I'll leave right away. I'm all finished here anyway. I'll see you in 25 minutes."

"Hey, that's great. Go to the flight-line; see Puffy at the control van. I'll be in my office and I'll see you there."

"OK, see ya!"

He sat for a moment wishing for a quick and simple solution to the problems that Dick had described. The flight had to go off as planned. A hell of a lot of work would go down the drain if they couldn't fix things; and fast!

Harry rushed to his car and drove at an excessive speed to the airbase at Indian Springs. After being waved through the gate by the guard, he drove to the Sandia office and parked his car. As he entered, he was startled by a figure barely visible in the dark room.

"Wow! You gave me a start there. I didn't expect to see you here."

"Yeah, I know!"

\* \* \* \* \*

Dutch Mitchell was in the rear of the van. He had just sent the monitor technician out for a smoke break. He busied himself with the screen and controls on the rack in front of him when Dick Tishman walked into the operations van at the air force base at H-hour minus sixty minutes. He looked around and saw that everyone was at their consoles.

"Puff, have you seen Harry?"

"No, Dick, I haven't seen him since yesterday."

"How about you, Dutch, was he at the flight line?"

"Sorry, Dick, haven't seen him."

"Boy, that's strange, Harry has never missed an operation. I called him and asked him to check out the detection devices and then meet me here."

Dick sat down at his console, put on his headset, and started his checkout procedures. He was having difficulties with his instrumentation and called Puffy,

"I'm not getting all my readings on my dummy instrumentation package and I think we should cancel the hop."

"No way, Jose, you know the rules. We're the primary, and if we're OK, we go."

"I think you're wrong, Puff, our data is as important as yours, and we should wait for the next shot."

"My call hot shot and, by the way, why did you change the parameters of the flight?"

"I called Dutch, and changed it back to the original game plan."

"Is that right, Dutch, did he call, do we have the correct overlay on the plotting board?"

"That's affirm, boss, you're all set."

"Well, we're out of time. I've got to get the bird airborne."

As Puffy turned the drone on its final heading, CHARLIE ONE got on the air,

"FOX, CHARLIE ONE, we don't seem to be lined up properly. We're too far southwest and closer to ground zero."

"CHARLIE ONE, this is FOX, I show us right down the middle."

"FOX, from where I sit, we're too close and it looks a little hairy. I'm not visually lined as usual on Shoshone Mountain; I'm more than a skosh to port."

"CHARLIE, I show us right on, but you guys get out of there, balls to the wall."

"Roger that, FOX. We're out of here, CHARLIE TWO, let's haul ass."

Seconds after H-hour, all of Puffy Spearson's instruments went to zero.

"Dutch, did we have a power failure?"

"Negative, Boss, power is OK."

"Shit, I think we lost the bird."

"For the record, I told you to cancel."

"For the record, my ass. You're a real shithead, Dick."

"Fuck you, Puffy."

"I don't have time for this now ... CHARLIE, you guys OK?"

"That's affirm, FOX, but visibility in this shit is impossible."

"Understand, CHARLIE, but as soon as you can, we need a search. I think we may have lost the bird."

'FOX, CHARLIE TWO, I think I see pieces of the bird falling to the ground, not much left, but it all may be debris from the blast."

"CHARLIE, FOX, see if you can pinpoint the fallout, assuming it's the bird, and then come home."

"WILCO, FOX, returning to base."

As they left the van to attend the debriefing, Puffy shoved Tishman a little, still angry at his bitching. Tishman stayed behind momentarily and made a copy of the air-ground voice audiotape. A few moments later, he left the van.

# PART 2

# HARRY AND SARAH

---

*NOVEMBER 1, 1992: PHILADELPHIA, PENNSYLVANIA*

Max and Oz sat facing each other at the diner having their weekly off-the-diet breakfast. Coffee, in white thick navy mugs, was half gone as Mary set the creamed chip beef and home fries with onions in front of Oz, and the crisp bacon and eggs under Max's nose. Mary smiled at the two retired guys that she had been serving for several years. Both looked fit, probably due to the insistence of their wives and physicians that they exercise frequently at a gym. They were of average height and Oz was the heavier of the two. What Mary noticed most was that they smiled and laughed a lot, with each other, her and anyone else nearby. She guessed that they were in their sixties and it was obvious that they had been good pals for a very long time.

Max, through a mouthful of toast,

"Listen, Oz, this is a good engaging opening. It ain't exactly like Sartre with his 'Mother died today.', but it will catch your eye, don't ya think?"

"Yeah, sure! We're not doing great literature here, Max, all we got to do is make up a two or three page invitation to the reunion. I think the last page should be a reservation form, like something they can fill out and then return to us with a check."

"OK, I get the drift, but I wanted to sort of create a tone and get a feel for it."

"Yep. You always did like to get a feel; go ahead."

Oz listens as Max reads.

"Hey, I like that pace and tone."

"Are you mocking me?"

"No, I'm mocking the counterman. Go on, give me some more tone and pace."

Mary spilled some more coffee into the two cups as Max wiped the last of the yolk off his plate with his toast.

"Oz, are we sure we want to get into this and do you really want to meet all the old frat guys this summer?"

"Sure we do! It'll be fun. And it won't be much work. Look. I bumped into 'Bloomy' and he says he and Jake Polish have been starting to arrange for an informal get together during this summer, like over a quiet weekend."

"Yeah, and?"

"So I told him that we could help out and he knew I was up on computer stuff, so I volunteered us to do the invitations and hotel reservation information, collect the checks and sort of coordinate things on the computer."

"Hey, I'm not getting involved in dealing with hotels and things."

"No, no. The other guys will deal with that. I think it's the Nittany Lion Inn, we'll only pass on the checks to them; or even have the returned form and check sent directly to 'Bloomy'. How's that?"

"All right. So what about the search for guys that they have no addresses for?"

"I can help by searching the Internet and maybe find some of the guys for them. C'mon we'll have fun. We haven't been up there for years and it'll be with the girls, like old times."

"You convinced me, already. Hey, Mary, can we get an ashtray and another shot of what passes for coffee around here?"

Oz and Max, breakfast finished, kibitzed the bald guy at the diner's cash register, and headed for Oz's car at the curb.

"Oz, remind me who Jake Polish is from the frat in State College, I can't remember anything except his name."

"He was Bobby Smitz's roommate for a few years. He was the guy who bought the first Fiat we ever saw. Remember the story? He gets Bobby to drive him to Pittsburgh to the Fiat dealer and the salesman is going down the list of options taking down the order. The last thing he asks Jake is does he want a radio and Jake pipes-up, "No, what do I need a radio for? I don't understand Italian!""

"Yeah, right!—I *do* remember that; He was kidding wasn't he?"

## *JANUARY, 1952: STATE COLLEGE, PENNSYLVANIA*

Harry Connors and Dick Tishman had been friends at the frat for three years. Harry had grown up in State College and began at Penn State as a freshman. Dick, about the same build as Harry, but stiffer had a ruddy complexion and always had a ready smile; a bit too ready for some tastes! Dick was from Philadelphia and spent his first year as a freshman center in Swarthmore, PA. His next three years were spent on campus. They were fraternity brothers and although they were never roommates, they became rather close. Some classes were taken together, squash and basketball were common efforts and most of their outdoor time together was spent hiking the trails around Nittany Mountain looking for fossils, Indian artifacts, horns and bones. Tishman always would be in Harry's debt, for Harry performed a task, considered by all 'in the know', above and beyond the ingenuity of most.

It was during their junior year and the Miss Penn State contest was being held. At the finals, Tishman's girlfriend, not pinned, but almost, was one of the five finalists. At a time when only tall, thin, light complexioned blondes won such contests; Carla was a tanned, dark haired, five-foot one-inch

-ALTS

beauty with large, seductive dark eyes. The finals were held in an overcrowded 'Rec' hall and the finalists, dressed in their wonderful gowns, sat on stage. The MC explained that he would introduce each young woman while they remained seated and he would hold his hand over each as he mentioned their names. At the mention of their name, the audience applause would be registered on a sound meter. The process was simple and took only several minutes. Each pretty girl received loud clapping, hollers and yipping from the crowd and at the end, it was clear that the meter's pointer slammed against the high side of its oval face assuring Carla of her win. Tishman went wild, whooping and jumping at his seat at the front of the auditorium. Crowns were placed, awards presented and the jubilant attendees slowly emptied the hall. At breakfast the next day, usually late on Sunday mornings, Dick Tishman entered the frat dining room with a big smile, walked to Harry Connors and planted a big wet and loud kiss on his cheek. Everyone in the room stood and applauded a master. All 'in the know' knew that Harry, saying that a good acoustics course would certainly be helpful one day, had made a 35 cent purchase at the 5 & 10 cent store on Allen Street on Saturday morning. By doing so he had assured Carla's victory. His purchase was a small metal dog whistle. When blown with gusto, it produces a very strong, high frequency blast unheard by human ears, but perceived very well by a sound meter!

*NOVEMBER 5, 1992: PHILADELPHIA, PENNSYLVANIA*

Sitting inside the Old City Café on Church Street, Max and Oz were talking over their coffee. They sat at a table near the front steam-covered windows overlooking the narrow, Belgian-blocked lane.

"So, how's the searching for the missing fraternity brothers going?"

"Not bad, actually, they gave me about fifteen, eighteen names and I've already got nine of them found."

"How did you do that so fast?"

"Easy so far. The Internet has several search methods and I got good hits on the first one I tried. Some of the names had several listings and I sent E-mail notes asking them if they are the ones from Penn State and in about two hours one night I got most of the answers back. There was one that we're looking for that's a bit strange."

"How so?"

"Well, once I verify that a guy is one of ours, I answer the E-mail and include a list of 'unknowns'."

"OK, so?"

"So one of the guys I had found let me know not to bother trying to find Harry Connors, 'cause he's dead."

"Oh, another one. You trying to ruin my meager breakfast?"

"No, no, that's not the point. Sure, we're old enough that some of us aren't around anymore, but this one is strange. I mean this guy said he saw an obit in the Alum magazine or somewhere about Harry and he keeps those things in his mailing files."

"What kind of files?"

"He said he kept a college mailing list file, something he did for his business. You know, he sent frequent mail-outs and one of his lists were Penn State people. Don't ask me what for, 'cause he didn't say, OK?"

"OK. Why is this strange? I don't get it."

"The guy said that the thing sounded a little strange that's all. Anyway, I asked him to find it and fax it to me. I'll show it to you when I get it."

"Yeah, good, thanks. Hey, I got the reunion notices with the form that you suggested, and I'm ready to mail out the first batch. As you feed me more names, I'll send out more."

"Will do. Say; let's run to the hardware store on Fourth

Street and then over to the ATM. I need to make a deposit and get some cash for the weekend."

"Good enough. I'm finished here."

As they walked out of the warm coffee shop, they headed toward Second Street and Max began to tell Oz a story. They were both chuckling and had their arms around each other's shoulders as they rounded the corner and headed for their car.

### *JUNE, 1952: STATE COLLEGE, PA*

Harry's last semester at Penn State was both wonderful and wondrous. He knew he walked on air and seemed in a daze. Oh, yeah, he was in what several of the experts called 'true love euphoria' or, 'I can't imagine that anything could feel like this!' He had been dating Sarah for about a year. They met in an English Literature Class and found that they were both enthralled with Dylan Thomas and very quickly with each other. They never knew if it was 3 o'clock and they spent one hour together or 1 o'clock and they spent three hours together

This happened about the time Dick Tishman and Carla went their separate ways. Dick had always claimed that Carla's inane blathering would drive him nuts and Carla, bless her candid soul, just called Dick a dishonest, untrustworthy, un-adulterated bastard! At any rate, Dick dated someone different every week and seemed unscathed by the parting of his former beloved.

Sarah and Harry spent their spare time walking in the woods, going to Whipple's Dam and, while sticking their feet in the water, talked and talked. Movies at the 'Armpit' on Allen Street and a big cheeseburger with Swiss cheese at the 'Skeller' on Pugh Street was their usual Friday night date. Sarah was not a local, like Harry, and she always asked about the town. They were sitting on the short wall on College Avenue watching the cars and a bunch of other kids go by.

"Harry, how come you stay at the frat house on Hamilton Street when your mom lives just a few blocks down on Foster?"

"She's smart, I guess, always thinking about me, of course. She just thought that it would be better for me living out of the house. You know, being independent and all. She confessed to me once that she had the best of it, 'cause I was out of the house going to college, but I was close enough to see her often."

"She's great, and your Dad's been dead for a long time, huh?"

"Hmm, yeah. She never went out with anyone else that I know of. She likes her job at the college and the extra money she gets by renting the third floor of the house really helps out."

"Who's up there, on the third floor?"

"Right now, a married couple—he's working on his Ph.D. in some Mineral Industries and his wife, I think, is a secretary on campus. My mom told me that she's going to have a baby in about six or seven months and they were worried about keeping the apartment. Mom told them not to worry, that she would love to have a baby in the house."

"How come the movie house is called the 'Armpit'?"

"Hah! I don't know when it started or who started it, but they had a coal heater in the basement and during the winter when all the windows are shut and the heat can't be regulated too well, so it gets pretty steamy in there. The coal smell, when it's burning gives off some kind of sulfur smell. During the summer they keep all the windows open and they're on Allen Street. My buddy Steve lives in the Metzger building that faces the 'Armpit' and he told me that he hears all the sound tracks of all the movies all summer long."

Curfew at the dorms was 1 AM on Friday and Saturday nights. They got into the habit of walking to the dorms by way of Calder Alley, instead of the brightly-lit College Avenue.

Hand-in-hand, they would stroll and at every slightly darkened area they would stop and, very slowly and tenderly, kiss.

* * * * *

A friend of Harry's at the frat was a weird one. Phil was from a Pittsburgh suburb and always had a hard salami hanging in his closet. Late at night, after working at his desk, he would cut off a bug hunk of the thing and if it was autumn, he'd have a gallon jug of apple cider hanging out the window on a short rope. He was a 'half-assed' chemistry major who learned that if you cover the mouth of the jug of the local-grown cider with cheese cloth and let it sit, it would naturally stew, fuss and bubble. After a month or so, the fermentation would produce a mild and cheap source of booze. A quirk of Phil's was to leave his alarm clock set on weekend mornings. He was easily pleasured by the fact that he would be awakened, go pee, and return to bed to, as he put it, " . . . be in the arms of Morpheus for three more hours." He slept 'til almost noon every Saturday and Sunday.

Phil's family had a little fishing and hunting cottage near the little town of Bald Eagle, only about 15 to 20 miles west of Penn State. It wasn't used very much and Phil had a key.

Harry and Sarah had been dating for about 6 months and had never been away together. Other than some gentle petting, their relationship remained what the authors in the Lit class called 'pure.' Harry suggested some time away from campus and Sarah agreed. Phil, always crazy, but always trustworthy, gave them his key to his folks' place after he made some calls to make sure it was going to be vacant. Sarah, a week ahead of time, signed out for the weekend at the housemother's office at her dorm, a necessary and formal requirement of the institution. The two took off in a borrowed, beat-up English Crosly and stopped at a grocery store in Port

Matilda on their way. They found the place easily, for Phil had said that, "Chemistry guys make damn good maps!"

The two days were spent happily, quietly and alone. They made simple meals together, walked the woods with the Bald Eagle mountain range as a backdrop. The weather was perfect and just holding hands, they both agreed, was grand. They spent two nights together, in the same bed, with only touching and holding each other. Both nights, they talked forever and fell asleep, smiling, in each other's arms. On Sunday morning, still in bed their bodies entwined, Sara asked,

"I loved how we slept together, but didn't sleep together. Was it OK?—I mean was it all right if we didn't—you know."

"Of course it was OK. OK?—God, it is glorious just to be with you."

"I mean, is it something I didn't do or anything? Harry, I need to go very slow—this kind of thing is all new to me, and I know I love you, and—"

"Hush. It's perfectly all right. You know I love you and we have the rest of our lives together. Why not just say that we had nocturnal omissions this weekend, OK?"

"That's one of the big reasons that I love you, you know?"

That weekend was like a key that locked them together for life. On the short ride back to campus they planned the 'death do us part' deed and smiled all the way toward State College.

\* \* \* \* \*

Three or four days a week Harry would walk off campus the short distance to Graham's and pick up the Times and go across the street to the Corner Room. This break was needed to keep mind, heart and body in good shape, for he would join a friendly group of pals in one of the large window booths overlooking Allen Street. Everything was discussed with passion, humor, energy, and often a huge measure of bullshit.

Like the time that Harry, Dick, Steve, two girls named Betsy and Eunice argued about Dick's take on Einstein's theory of relativity. Dick claimed that, given the theory, if a dog chased its tail faster and faster, in an ever decreasing circle, it would eventually disappear up its own asshole! Needless to say, the ensuing, loud discussion prompted the manager to ask the group to give up the booth, for others were waiting. Humph to him!

Harry, leaving through the revolving door, headed toward Foster Street on his way to visit his mother.

### NOVEMBER 9, 1992: PHILADELPHIA, PENNSYLVANIA

Max and Oz were driving south on Delaware Avenue on their way to Home Depot to look at some mirrors. They had had breakfast and Oz had given Max the fax about Harry Connors.

"You got this from Phil Marsh, right?"

"Yeah, like I said, it came from the Alum Magazine."

"I can see why this would intrigue somebody. It says here that Harry's presumed death happened in Nevada in 1953 and this blurb is dated 1960"

"Right."

"Then it mentions our fraternity, his degree information and that he was survived by his wife and no name given or whereabouts."

"I remember, clearly, that he was dating that cute little gal, Sally, Sarah, Shirley something."

"Hell, I remember her, it was Sarah. I even recall that they talked about getting married after they got out of State. And what is this stuff about 'presumed'?"

"Well, this I questioned also."

"Also you qvestioned, maybe?"

"Very funny, you wanna listen, or what?"

"Sure."

"I called Phil and he didn't know anything else, all he did was clip the thing from the magazine and that's it."

"Why does he do that, you know, date and keep things like that on file?"

"Who knows, maybe he had trouble with his toilet training! I remember his frat room. Everything was in place and all his clothes were neat and hung up like his mother was going to do an inspection. Nice guy, but too neat."

"So then what?"

"I make a few calls to some of the guys, and by the way, some of them are astonished that nobody's killed you yet, with your wise-ass mouth."

"They're all jealous of my wit and charm."

"Oh, yeah!—so I eventually get to Dick Tishman. I find him on the Internet and he's listed in Princeton, New Jersey. We shoot the breeze for a couple of minutes and then I ask about Harry. He seems a little uncertain and then tells me that the blurb is correct. Probable is the correct word, because Harry disappeared in Nevada in 1963, and catch this—when both of them were working together doing some research stuff during atomic explosions. Both of them!"

"Wow! What else?"

"He said he felt bad about not keeping in touch with Sarah, and yes, they were married at the end of '52 and she was out there with Harry, living temp-like in Las Vegas. Dick said she went back to State College to live and she had a little boy."

"Why does everyone say that someone had a little girl or a little boy?"

"What the hell you talking about?"

"When somebody has a baby boy or girl, they're always little, aren't they?"

"Please, spare me your razor sharp wit, will ya? He tells me something else."

"What?"

"He tells me that my call to him and mentioning Harry is a coincidence, because Harry's son called him and even visited him recently with the son's girl friend."

"What was that all about, did he say?"

"Sure, because I asked. He told me that they are trying to find out what happened to Harry."

"Hey, now that is interesting. A mystery from almost forty years ago and now a son looking to see what he could find. Anyway, what's Dick doing now?"

"He's a retired Professor, you know, one of the emeritus things. He said he was up at Princeton for twenty years or so. He's a pretty smart guy. I remember reading a bunch of years ago about him getting some high class Physics award."

"You mean like the Nobel thing?"

"No, not that, but something high up there. I told him that I was going to get back to him and maybe we would drive up there sometime to say hello. He didn't sound too receptive, and he said that he didn't think he was interested in attending our get-together in State College."

"That doesn't surprise me, huh, you?"

### JUNE, 1952: SANDIA CORPORATION, NEW MEXICO

At graduation time Dick had his degree in Physics and Harry won his BSEE in Electrical Engineering with a minor in Biology. They were lucky and got jobs at the same place. Sandia Corporation was the production engineering section, referred to as the "Z" division, of the Atomic Energy Commission (AEC) located near Albuquerque, New Mexico. The name derived from the notable nearby mountain known for its wonderful winds and drafts that drew hot air balloonists to its heights. In 1952, when the new grads started there, AT&T Bell system directed the Sandia Labs. The lab functions were to develop and make formal the mysterious art of nuclear weapons, create protocol manuals, act as the nation's repository for U.S. stockpiles, and the actual assembly of the weapons.

As the new employees became familiar with their new positions, and their new shared bachelor quarters, they learned that each of the Armed Services had their own projects associated with the development of nuclear warfare and peripheral projects. One such project involved the U.S. Navy's work developing procedures for the delivery of weapons by aircraft. The project managers and control group was a Navy experimental squadron dubbed, "VX-4" at Point Mugu, California. Dick and Harry were becoming acclimated to their new projects, meeting all the people with whom they would work, finding out where the men's room was and other equally important facets of the lab. The Navy had started work on the development of several aircraft drones as an integral part of their project. The object was to convert several Douglas AD Skyraiders into craft that could be flown manually and/or by remote control outside the cockpit, namely, on the ground or by a chase plane.

On their off time and with a new environment to be appreciated and investigated, the new, 'New Mexicans' began to hike and search for 'history', as they referred to it, in the mountains and desert. In the next few months, and in heat that would boil your rear end, they roamed, scampered and climbed through Laguna and Acoma reservations to the west and northward in Jemez Canyon. In the latter, they found some great Arrowheads near San Filipe Reservation. Dick wanted to keep what they had found but Harry prevailed by convincing Dick to merely take some shots with their Kodak and turn the artifacts in at the Reservation office.

In the meantime, the Commanding Officer of VX-4, received orders to send an experimental detachment to the Naval Air Experimental Station (NAES) at the Naval Base in Philadelphia. Three AD Skyraiders were on their way there for the conversion to pilot-less aircraft or drones. Lt. Comdr.

'Puffy' Spearson was to lead the group. Their main purpose was to the convert the planes and to take all the bugs out of the control systems, plan experiments to see how close an aircraft can be to a detonation without harm, measure and evaluate the results of the blast and most importantly the radiation levels.

VX-4 would be in good company at the small Naval Air Station at the Base in Philly, for there they would meet other groups involved in Carrier catapult testing and development, structural testing of new craft and materials, all highly classified. They would not want for intellectual competition. Puffy, a World War II vet who came to the navy from the Merchant Marines, got his moniker because he seemed to have a cigar in his mouth most of the time. Most people swore that he merely slid the stogy to the side of his mouth at mealtime so he could eat without removing it. Spearson was loud, bombastic, filled with high energy and built like a tall fire-plug. His men feared him a bit and respected his knowledge and direction. Among others in his technical group were Lt. Bert Foley, and Lt.jg B.K. Kelly. Both were trusted and able pilots, familiar with the Douglas aircraft and trained as manual and remote pilots for the drone.

By the end of August, Harry and Dick were deep into several projects. The most pressing was work on a new trigger device, which could be ground or air-controlled and miniaturized radio devices for immediate and radio-relayed evaluation of radiation levels. A few days before Labor Day, their supervisor, Jim Falconer, a Ph.D.-type called them in his office.

"Morning, guys, I wanted you both in here first thing this AM 'cause I've got news."

"God forbid, a raise so early in our career? Or are we to have a week off with pay?"

"You wish! But actually I think you'll both like this deal."

"Spill it, James, boss."

"The Navy is interested in some of the stuff we've got here and they're doing some hush-hush experimental work. Some of what you two are working on can be helpful to them. They wanted me, and two others to go, but the Chief said no, So we're sending you guys. You're new and somewhat expendable here for a while, but it will be good experience for you guys."

"Please tell us that this is not a permanent transfer to Nome, Alaska or like that?"

"Much better than that, you both are from Philadelphia, right?"

"Dick is from Philly and I'm from about 200 miles from there—from State College, where Penn State is. What about Philly?"

"The Naval Base, actually, it says the Naval Air Base in Philly. Where the hell is that?"

"That's in South Philly. What's the deal?"

"A naval liaison officer will prime you this afternoon. He's coming in soon to see the Chief. The short of it is a temporary duty change . . a few months down there and then a possible move again or back here, I don't know. You guys gather up your work on the trigger and the radiation-detection projects, get clearance for the files and lockup briefcases for your wrists. After your briefing with the navy guy, clean out your workstations and I'll have the personnel office put in storage anything you leave behind in your apartment."

"Hell, what's the rush?"

"You guys know what the Navy says?"

"No, what?"

"If you stand still, you'll get painted!"


*SEPTEMBER, 1952: PHILADELPHIA NAVAL BASE*

Harry and Dick arrived in Philadelphia early in the month with the few clothes they owned and twenty-three pounds of classified files. Their research gear was to follow ASAP on a Military Air Transport System aircraft, under guard.

They were lucky, for they didn't have to worry about where to stay, and Harry was concerned that Dick would drag him to live with Dick's parents. The Navy gave them space in the bachelor officer's quarters right in the middle of the navy base. The base was a sprawling area at the south end of Broad Street in South Philly that extended from there to the west almost to the eastern approach of the Philadelphia airport. On the base was the small Naval Air Station where the two of them would do most of their work.

While unpacking in their new quarters, Dick made a fast call to his folks and they insisted that he visit that night.

"Hey, Harry, my parents insist that we go up there tonight."

"Hell, friend, I'm beat and I don't have any clean clothes."

"I'm bushed too, but let's get it out of the way and, anyway, maybe I can get my mom's car. She hardly uses it and it would be a benefit to the entire city to get her off the road for as long as we're here. We're the same size, you know, and you've borrowed my stuff before, right?"

"OK, that'll do and I take it your mom's not exactly a marvelous driver?"

"Are you kidding? I love her and all, but she's an accident going somewhere to happen! Luckily, she alerts everyone in a two-block radius of her arrival."

"How so?"

"You'd have to hear it to believe it, but her gear-meshing noises trying to get from one gear to another could wake up the dead."

Dick took Harry to his parent's home in Oak Lane that night for the obligatory 'we haven't seen you for an age son', supper. Harry, accustomed to small towns and easy access to most everything, was in a bit of a transportation shock. He was still reeling from the flight from New Mexico, which involved three planes. Now, Dick led him out of the Base, on a bus north on Broad Street to Snyder Avenue, down the steps to the subway, a twenty-minute noisy, screechy, bouncing ride. During the ride, Dick shouted over the noise making like a tour guide.

"I think that Broad Street is one of the longest, straightest streets in America at about 12 miles."

"Wow, this is loud down here, how much longer?"

"Just a few more minutes. I used to use these subways every school day to get to and from home. That was when I went to High School."

"I'm glad I lived in a place where I could walk to school."

"Nah, you get used to it and, really, ya never even think about it. We're pretty close to Olney Avenue now, hang on."

The subway screamed to a jolting halt that almost threw Harry to the floor, saved only by his fast grabbing onto a pole near the door. He trailed Dick up steps that seemed like four flights and onto a trolley car for, thankfully, only ten minutes or so.

"God, I think I'm getting dizzy. Some food will certainly help."

"Hey, what my mom lacks in driving skills she makes up in her culinary expertise, you're going to love it."

They walked for just a couple of blocks and up the few steps to a modest row home, typical of this section of town. Hugs, kisses, introductions were joyous and warm. Harry was immediately made welcome and made an unofficial member of the family. The dinner was great, for anything other than mess hall food was bound to be terrific. The banter at the dinner table was fun, caring and Harry felt comfortable being there.

"So, Pop, how do you like this new house now that you and Mom are here for almost a year?"

"Well, it's not Moyamensing Avenue, but we're happy here and the neighbors are swell."

"I'll sort of miss the old neighborhood. I'm not quite used to it up here."

"Yeah, all you kids got along real well—do you remember going to the 'swimmies' on Third Street with all your friends?"

"Oh, yeah, I got dunked plenty there, but they did really teach us how to swim well."

"So, I know that we can't ask you what you're doing here at the Navy Yard, but we can call you there?"

"Sure you can, and you can leave a message with the duty guy and I'll call you. Harry and I will be busy, but we'll come for supper when we can, right, Harry?"

"Sure, anytime we can—the dinner is delicious, by the way, Mrs. Tishman."

"So, Pop, everything is OK at work?"

"Of course, sure."

"and you're sarrisfied?"

Mr. Tishman, with a broad grin,

"Yes, I'm very sarrisfied."

"And you, Richard, you got money?"

"Yes, I'm OK."

"You're sure, you know, enough to be really OK, for sure?"

"Honest, Pop, I've got plenty!"

"Good, then send me some!"

Dick's dad laughed at his old familiar joke and all enjoyed each other's company.

Dick got the loan of his mother's car for the duration of his stay in Philly. The ride back to the base was only about 25 minutes and a heck of a lot more comfortable. Both of them fell into their beds almost immediately after they got to their quarters. The long journey, the excitement about the projects, the anxiety of their responsibilities and the huge supper did them in. The young men, atop their light blankets, fell into the kind of slumber that doesn't include sugarplums, but the shapes were vaguely the same.

———

＊ ＊ ＊ ＊ ＊.

Although Harry had visited the city several times, he was not all that familiar with the place and Dick had promised to show him around as soon as they got the chance.

The following morning after meeting with the project chiefs, they had a short conference with Puffy Spearson. He seemed like a gruff, but nice guy and after about five minutes you could decipher his Alabama speech passed through his cigar like he was always sneering at something. In close quarters, that big fat hunk of tobacco could throw up smoke clouds that encompassed half the space and render the ceiling invisible.

Puffy, the other pilots and a few of their senior crew, and the new guys reviewed their present needs and the hurry up timetable of the main projects.

At 11 AM, Puffy suggested getting some chow and he, Harry and Dick piled into Puffy's Ford convertible. Passing through the north gate onto Broad Street, Puffy got thrown a smart salute from the Shore Patrolman. All he got back was a wave and a loud 'harumph' from Puffy. Five minutes later, the boys were introduced to the Melrose Diner where they were called 'deary', had chipped beef on toast and plenty of coffee. Puffy even grabbed the check. Harry and Dick soon learned that Puffy was very generous, for when he had some cash, everyone got drinks, food and anything else that was available. Harry and Dick had particularly liked the dessert that Puffy suggested, the hot apple pie with vanilla sauce. Overstuffed, they returned to the base and began setting up their projects and work routines.

Over the next few weeks, they worked hard and diligently during the day, sometimes to seven or eight in the evening. At night, as often as they could, they played equally as diligently. Harry and Sarah talked, by phone, every day, even if it was only for a few minutes. They saw each other often, mostly on weekends and at times double-dated with Dick and a date. He, in his words, was still playing the field. He seemed to be interested superficially, at least, with several young women. Sarah and Harry were planning a small wedding sometime at the end of the year. They seemed to be in a constant state of ecstatic, which Sarah claimed, was just east of New Jersey. During the week, in the evenings when they could get away, the guys would go into town, only ten or twelve minutes by car. The weather was still pleasant, for Fall was great in the city. The summer heat and humidity was gone and, usually, a cool "Indian summer" treated the locals to beautiful weather. Harry and Dick, seated without their sport coats on, were having dinner at Pop Edwards on Market Street. Harry had been there before and fell in love with the hot pastrami on rye. The sauerkraut with it wasn't bad, either. This was a bar that had beers from several places all over the world and any one of them was a good dancing partner with the overfilled sandwich.

"We have the radiation devices and their arrays settled, right?"

"As far as I'm concerned, we're fine. My team says we're ahead of schedule and we have the dummy model almost finished. All the radio transmitters are in place with temporary securing clips, you know, just in case we want to change them after the first few tests. One of the team guys painted the face of Charlie Chaplin on the dummy. The visiting Admiral from D.C. didn't appreciate that very much."

"What do ya mean?"

"Well, this group of inspection people from Washington pulls an unannounced look-see and this big brass with an obvious weed up his grommet heads them up."

"And?"

"He gets a look at the Charlie face and gets red all over and gave us all a lecture about this isn't the time nor place for levity and all that stuff. Hell, we're busy enough without having to hang our heads and do twelve mea culpas every time some hotshot comes in for a tour."

"Go easy, pal, you'll choke on your pastrami."

"Yeah, well, we'll be hitting all the deadlines way ahead of schedule and those guys can kiss my derriere!"

"Right, and our stuff with the radio controls and conjunction relays for the ground controls is OK too. You tired, or do you want to grab another beer someplace else?"

"I'm not tired, yet, let's get another drink around the corner."

The boys each dropped a dollar on the table, slid out of the booth over which dozens of old Philadelphia pictures hung, and paid their checks at the bar. Paul, behind the bar, smiled and waved them a goodbye as they went out onto Market Street.

For a weekday night, Billy Kretchmer's, on Ranstead Street, was fairly crowded. It was about 10 PM and the long bar on the right had half the barstools occupied. Beyond the bar, the room opened a bit and a third of the tables had a few couples listening to Billy on clarinet and his friends on piano and bass. Thelonius Monk's, 'Round About Midnight', in Billy's hand was, indeed, something to hear and enjoy. My, my; it was very tasty, indeed.

### OCTOBER, 1952: PHILADELPHIA NAVAL BASE

Work had been hectic for almost two months at the Air Station. Several AD Skyraider aircraft were almost completed. Their capability as drones would be ready for testing in two days, at most. Harry, Dick and the teams of other units had double-checked all electronic controls, radar effectiveness, remote devices, radiation detection devices, transmitters and receivers. Every patch cord, cable, connector—everything except their skivvies were scrutinized until all the guys complained of double vision. All teams and maintenance groups worked late at least three days a week and, without much complaining, they had also worked every other Saturday.

At an early meeting during the last week of October, Puffy stood before the group of senior team leaders and project coordinators. On a large display screen behind him was a hand-written, large schedule clearly specifying a proposed protocol for the testing and evaluation that would take the better part of the following three to four weeks.

"Listen up guys! The smoking lamp is lit. At a protocol development meeting last night, several of us wound up at Fedullo's bar and came up with a tentative schedule."

"What's the timetable look like now?"

"Yesterday at 1430 I received a heads-up from the C.O. and it was fairly clear that it was more than a mere heads-up."

"What's the poop?"

"We have, at most, a month or so to wind up this thing and we will probably remain as a group and be moved to a more secure test site."

"Where are we talking about?"

"Geez, I don't know, and what the hell's the difference. Wherever it is, they say go, and we go, right? Just for the record, all in unison, now:"

"Ours is not to question why, ours is just to do or die!"

"Very good, guys, we're all in good voice. First, I'd like to commend publicly our new young blood-additions. They came here as virgins. New jobs, new place, new faces and all the baggage that shit comes with. They hopped on the wagon when it was going half-speed and helped immediately to get us up to full go!"

"Rah, rah! OK, get on with the show."

"All right, spoilsport. Harry, you first."

"Dick and I and our crews came up with the following: Washington definitely does not want us to fly our drones any-where near Philly or any well-populated area without a pilot on board. So, here's what we propose: the first step will be a strictly manual flight consisting of takeoff, flight and landing. The second stage will be a manual takeoff and landing with the flight being controlled on the ground and/or the chase plane. The next group of short tests will involve takeoff and flight by remote control and if that goes OK, we'll quickly add the remote landing. At all times, Puffy will be in radio and radar contact with Bert Foley, B.K. Kelly, and Byron Peterson."

"What back-up controls, does the pilot on board have, you know, for emergencies?

"Dick?"

"A 'kick-off' control is installed so that the drone pilot can remove all the remotes with one simple fast action sever-switch. We actually found it easier to do this by way of a small foot switch."

"If the aboard pilot perceives anything about to go awry he kicks the switch and takes immediate control."

"How 'bout if ground or chase control wants to reverse things?"

"Easy. We've got a three-way servo-system so that any of the three controllers, Fox, Able or Charlie, can move easily from control to no control."

"That's super! So if poor 'B.K.' passes out from too much night-before beer, we can glide his ass down to the "Doc" on the ground. Hey, I like it!"

*NOVEMBER, 1952: PHILADELPHIA, PENNSYLVANIA*

It was Wednesday late morning and the teams at the Air Station had already put in 33 hours that week. Harry and Dick, in addition to their regular projects, had been asked to work with another group with an important, concurrent, project.

"Harry, the C.O. made it clear that, as busy as we were, we have to coordinate with these other guys"

"I understand, but our plates are full and a half."

"Yeah, I know, but it's logical to get us into their act, otherwise our set-up will bump into theirs and there could be some dreadful results."

"OK, Dick—you're going to take the brunt of it, so it's OK with me. How do you want to set things up?"

"Well, the problem they have, and I don't know anything except the basics yet, is our communications network regarding the drone, chase planes, ground control, radar monitoring, radiation receivers, transmitters and all our voice lines, must remain clean. And don't forget there's going to be several other planes, piloted, floating around with radiation and God knows what's in them to monitor the blasts. They have to be clean too."

"Clean, as in not producing spurious signals?"

"Right!"

"Then I assume that their advanced experimental trigger device is a frequency limited control that . . ."

"Don't ever assume anything and certainly let's not hypothesize. We'll have enough to do. They'll keep us in the dark for everything except exactly what we need to know. You can bet your ass that whenever we leave the base there will be somebody watching us some of the time."

"Listen, Dick, let's not mention about being watched to Sarah. She gets a little nervous about that stuff."

"Right, OK, I won't."

At noon, Puffy grabbed the two guys and herded them to his car.

"Men, I've been summarizing our work and the 'skinny' derived from our planning sessions to the brass every week and they are so thrilled that the scrambled eggs on their caps just shiver and shake."

"That's wonderful, when do we get our raises?"

"Just like you kids, always wanting more allowance. Get in and we'll go to Nick's, the least I can do is to buy you guys a great roast pork sandwich and a beer."

The drive up to Jackson Street was short and sweet. Puffy had the top down, it was 42 degrees and some leaves, falling off the old trees in South Philly, were drifting into the car. One got stuck on the lit end of Puffy's cigar and he almost drove them into a funeral parlor on Broad Street. This was fairly easy to do, for somebody once reported that there was an Italian funeral parlor for every three residents in South Philly. As Puffy backed up away from the funeral home,

"Hey, I just thought you guys wanted to stop here for a couple of cold ones!"

Later, devouring the juicy lunch, all three of them tried, desperately, to drip the juice into their napkins. Puffy, with a few drops on his chin,

"At my last meeting with the brass, after my report, they told me that we'll have just to early January to get this show on the road."

"Did they say where this road will go?"

"Nah, not yet, but it's got to be Nevada. They got test sites set up and it's unpopulated and all. Listen, when they tell me, then all you guys will know. Say, I'm going with a couple of the guys tonight to The Wedge, you know, Julie Gibson does her 'Dance of the Bride' and they got a nice little jazz group between her shows, want to go with?"

"That sounds good to me, how 'bout you, Harry?"

"Thanks, Puffy, but Sarah and I have concert tickets. I've been promising her to go to the Academy since we got here."

"Understood, young man, what are they putting on?"

"It's an Italian concert, an overture by Verdi and they're doing all of Vivaldi's Four Seasons—it should be good"

"Yeah, well, my favorite is Puccini's Filet Mignon."

\* \* \* \* \*

Sarah and Harry ate a quick dinner at the Automat and got to the Academy of Music on time. Their seats were up on the third balcony, but they could see and hear everything. They felt enormously excited, for everyone was dressed up and the folks in the orchestra seats were really 'spiffy'.

Afterwards, coming down the steps onto Broad Street,

"Sarah, do you want to catch some music at the Blue Note up on Ridge Avenue, are you tired or what?"

"I think I am, a little, Harry. Is it OK just to have some coffee and desert at the Harvey House?"

"Sure, anything you want."

Walking across Locust Street, Harry took Sarah's elbow.

"We'll probably be finished our work here soon and we'll get to someplace else to finish the projects that we're on."

"Where will you go?"

"I can't talk about it, but more important, we'll be married before I go and I hope that you'll come with me. It may only be for a short time, but I want you there with me, together. I told Dick that I'm through with him as a roommate, you're much prettier than he is."

"Of course I'll go with you. I wouldn't want it any other way."


### DECEMBER, 1952: PHILADELPHIA, PENNSYLVANIA

It was the first weekend in the month, and this Friday night had been planned for several weeks. Most of the guys from the base, their wives and girlfriends were present at a pre-wedding party for Sarah and Harry. Tishman and Spearson, both with dates, had been the master planners of this wondrous event at the Silver Lake Inn in New Jersey. Dinner and dancing overlooking the lake made for a pleasant evening. The lake, true to its name and with the help of a cold December moon, indeed made the water glistens as if there were lights just beneath the surface.

Harry held Sarah close as they danced comfortable and effortlessly to "Blue Tango."

"I can't believe we'll be married in a few days."

"Me, too, I'm excited like crazy!"

"Is there any word about when you might leave for the next place?"

"Nothing definite yet, but I'm sure we'll hear soon. Our work is essentially complete and it's just a matter of cleaning up some loose ends."

"I know you're concerned about our short honeymoon, but please don't concern yourself about it. What's important is that we'll be married and we can be together when you transfer to wherever."

"Well, as sure as you're OK with the thought of a quick weekend in Atlantic City. It's pretty cold this time of the year."

"Hey, you promised that we could get bundled up and take one of those rolling chair rides for the whole length of the boardwalk, right?"

"Yep, and the Traymore Hotel is supposed to be terrific. They promised a room with an ocean view."

"Mmmm, can't wait."

They left the dance floor as the band began to play 'Glow Worm' and joined the large table. As they approached their seats, Puffy's date, a buxom pretty gal from Passayunk Avenue took Harry's arm and led him back to the dance floor.

"Hey, I get to dance with the groom once, at least."

Puffy took the opportunity to take Sarah's arm and make like a pantomime bow at the waist and requested a dance with the bride-to-be.

Dick had noticed that Puffy had more than his share of booze, already, and that he seemed more like in a wrestling hold with Sarah and that he was smiling and talking directly into her left ear as she tried to separate from him. Dick got up quickly and tapped on Puffy's shoulder and pushed himself between the two.

"I'm cutting in here, Commander, shove off!"

"As you wish, young man—I'm for another drink, anyway."

"Sarah, are you OK?"

"Oh sure, he's so darn big and he's got something of a dirty mouth—I'm glad you came to the rescue, I really didn't like it. Please don't mention it to Harry, I don't think it's worth making a fuss over."

"Sounds good to me. How 'bout the four of us taking off and grabbing a nightcap someplace?"

"Good, let's get Harry away from what's-her-name and scram, the party's breaking up anyway."

Dick and his date Elaine, Sarah and Harry drove to Charlie Ventura's, found a small table in the darkened room and ordered drinks as Charlie, on stage, saxaphoned his marvelous way through 'Delicado'. This place had become one of their favorite spots, particularly on Saturday nights, for all the places in the city, except for private clubs, closed their bars down at midnight. It was great sometimes around closing time and many of the jazz people playing at other places and even in New York, would come to Charlie's and play until the wee hours. Anyone still there at closing was welcome to stay and just hang out and enjoy the extemporaneous music.

Driving back to town, the radio tuned to the 'Dawn Patrol', and the four of them listened to Jan Peerce sing 'The Bluebird of Happiness' for the umpteenth time and they still remained silent and smiling.

### DECEMBER 20, 1952: PHILADELPHIA NAVY BASE

Puffy Spearson stood behind a lectern facing the seated personnel of VX-4, NAES, Philadelphia, and the Sandia team. Harry and Dick had taken seats near one of the large windows. Dick was quietly stifling a yawn and Harry seemed to be in a daze as he stared eastward toward the Camden shipyards. Harry was grinning, for he was recalling how great the wedding was the weekend before and the wonderful time that he and Sarah had in Atlantic City. Harry's thoughts were, unfortunately, interrupted.

"Listen up, gentlemen. This morning's briefing is extremely important and will answer most of the questions we've had for the last few weeks. We have, this morning, Captain Alex McNair from Washington, representing the Director of Weapons Tests. He'd like to say a few words to you all before he meets with the CO here. Captain, it's all yours, Sir."

"Thank you Commander. Good morning to you all. First, I'd like to thank all of you for the tremendous jobs you've done here. All of us with the Weapons Tests Group are extremely pleased with the Four-Oh performance. We know that all of you are anxious to learn the where and what next. Here it is. The VX-4 group along with the Sandia experimental contingent will be transferred immediately to the Nevada Atomic Test Site. All pertinent equipment, aircraft, scientific gear will be removed from here and shipped at once. As you know, the Navy drone program will obtain weapons effect data concerning blast, thermal, radiation and other effects on combat personnel, aircraft and equipment. In addition, we are adding a great deal of important data to our level of knowledge in regard to Civil Defense concerns. All of you will become an important component of Exercise Desert Rock V. Specifically, you will be involved with Operation Upshot-Knothole, an atomic test series of eleven detonations that will take place from March 17th to June 4th, next. Now, I know you will have questions, but at this juncture, Commander Spearson will fill you in with some of the details. Thank you and good luck."

The Captain smiled and as he moved away from the lectern, a young aide standing at the door shouted,

"Attention on deck!"

---

The Navy people in the room jumped to their feet, at attention, as the officers left the room.

Puffy stood and came around in front of the platform and closer to the men. He perched on a corner of a small table.

"OK, guys, here's what I have so far. We will run our operations with the drones during at least five and maybe six detonations. All the blasts will be above ground and most will be ground zero atop towers. A couple will be air-drops. Specific drop dates are March 17, April 11, 18th and 25th, and May 8th. The drop-designations are 3,5,6,7,8 and, possible, number 9. The test series code names are respectively, Annie, Ray, Badger, Simon and Encore. The possible is named Grable."

"Hey, where the hell they get all these goofy names?"

"Who the hell knows? Listen up, there's more. The OP plan is as follows and I'll only go over a few things now. On all shots the AD drone, accompanied by an F8F mother ship and an F4D armed fighter, will operate at an altitude of 5000 feet above ground zero on a heading of 280 degrees True and at a distance of 6000 feet beyond ground zero at H-hour."

Bert Foley's head shot up; his frown was quite evident.

"Jesus, Puff, that's pretty damn close."

"It looks that way, Bert, but we've been assured that it will be safe."

"Oh, yeah, right!"

"Let me continue. Foley and Peterson, flying Charlie One and Two, will be as far away from the drone as they can while keeping it in sight. Kelly and Graves will be backup. In the event of an emergency with the drone control, the senior airborne drone control officer—that's you, Foley—is responsible for issuing the shootdown order."

"How big are the towers, any word on that?"

"Yeah, hold on, yeah, here—All of our shots are from 300-foot jobs, except one, and that's a 100-foot one. Oh, and by the way, the Encore shot will be a drop from a B-50 bomber flying at 19,000 feet."

"Oh, boy, I hope those guys know what they're doin'."

"Let's all pray they do, huh?"

"Harry, you and Dick and your teams will pack up your technical stuff and all the equipment for beta and gamma radiation detection, and the dummies. You'll get help from the base's labor pool. Guys, all of you know that their stuff is critical, for they have instrumented our dummy pilots so that the internal pilot hazards due to inhalation of fission products and other radioactive materials can be determined in the cockpit as the AD flies through the clouds. These guys will continue to coordinate with all other teams regarding communication details and accumulation, assimilation and analysis of data."

"Puff, do you have radiation expectation figures yet?"

"Right, I do, but let's call this meeting quits now. Please, everyone, all the details will be ironed out as of tonight and that includes moving schedules. Our ETA in Nevada is no later than the 30th of this month. Let's hustle our asses and to that end, ugh, no joke intended, all section leaders will meet with me in the small conference room in fifteen minutes. At that time all specifics in detail will be disseminated. At this moment, the personnel office is preparing transfer documents. Whoever asked about radiation expectations, well, there will be info sheets that all the section chiefs will get in the next hour or so. All pilots will get the go-no-go criteria now, but please remember that each operation will have a separate set of contingency plans for emergency situations. Now, let's get crackin'."

Dick and Harry headed for the coffee room and Dick said,

"I can pack in about ten minutes, call my folks and be out of here pronto. What are you and Sarah going to do?"

"We've got a week-to-week at the Essex Hotel on Filbert Street so it's easy to leave here."

"You were looking for a small apartment weren't you?"

"Yes, and am I glad we didn't commit ourselves to anything. Sarah will follow us as soon as I get a place for us. The hotel is a commercial little place and cheap for our purposes, but I'm sure she'll be happy to get out of there and out to Nevada. You ever been there?"

"No, but I think we'll be fairly close to Las Vegas. Maybe when we're not working our rears off, we can see the sights and also look into doing some digging out in the desert."

"Right, that would be fun. I bet there's lots of Indian stuff out there."

"I'm stopping at the head, I'll see you at the meeting."

*NOVEMBER 18, 1992: PHILADELPHIA, PENNSYLVANIA*

As usual, Oz picked up Max about 11 AM and a few moments later they were seated in one of the booths at the diner. Mary, typically, started to rattle off the specials for lunch, but her spiel was halted midway by a duet of,

"No, no, Mary, dear—just breakfast! Keep the lunch stuff."

After ordering, Max yells after Mary not to forget an ashtray as she heads for the kitchen.

"Listen, Oz, I dug up some background info on the Nevada area, just for the hell of it—you know, where Harry was working in '53."

"Yeah, huh-unh, so?"

"Marine Corps history journals in the library say that the 2nd Marine Air Corps Provisional Atomic Exercise Brigade, made up of guys from Camp LeJeune, North Caroline, were transported by Marine Air Group 16, from Cherry Point, NC and, with a refueling stop in Albuquerque, got to Nevada."

"What was the exercise, did it say?"

"Yeah, wait a minute, I got some more notes here. Yeah,

it says they went there to get familiar with conditions of atomic attack, and to test and develop tactics for putting helicopter forces close to the bomb blast. Another smaller group was to do radiological survey stuff and to study protection techniques against the blast and radiation."

"Hey, that's good, anything else?"

Breakfast, in the meantime, was placed in front of the guys with Mary's usual,

"Enjoy it, hon."

After a few gulps of more coffee and some of the waffles, Max unfolds another piece of paper and smiles.

"More notes—anyway, I went to the newspaper and asked a pal of mine to take a gander at his morgue, you know, like in the movies. He shows me how to run through the machine and look for stuff and it's real easy. I find a couple of interesting things. I'll read it: 'On a clear Saturday dawn of April 18, atop a 300-foot tower, an atomic bomb was detonated. It was one of the largest ever tested in the United States. 2200 Marines braced themselves while crouching in five-foot trenches, a mere 4000 yards from ground zero. At exactly 4:35 AM an enormously brilliant light illuminated the sky and everything under it. A dazzling bright orange reflection from a hellish fireball emerged and at the same time the earth shook making the trenches into serpentine alleys. A terrible blast was accompanied by waves of dust, dirt and debris that included rocks, vegetation and even animal parts, seemingly fried to a crisp. All this occurred within seven seconds and a klaxon sounded signaling the troops to rise from their positions in the trenches. A light purple-to-darker mushroom cloud was already at 4000 feet high and one mile wide. Some Marines advanced on foot under the atomic cloud; others landed in another sector by helicopter. Burning Joshua trees could be seen for miles. A small Marine neurological research team advanced into their area about 500 yards and were ordered to move quickly to the rear, for the radiation was 'too hot'. At 4:47 AM the troops . . ."

"OK, I get the picture, Max, finish your waffles and we'll talk in the car. You got some errands to run? Maybe, we get the errands out of the way and we can catch a movie."

### DECEMBER 28, 1952: DESERT ROCK, NEVADA

Most of the members of the VX-4 and the Sandia group were busy setting up their gear and unpacking those things that would remain here. All other field reception gear would be placed appropriately before each operation. Some of the group was over at Indian Springs, setting up the operation vans.

"Harry, what did you find in town this morning?"

"I got everything settled in quick order, for a change. These people out here are very cordial and helpful."

"So, what did you accomplish?"

"Well, everything, I guess. I found a real cute apartment very near the main drag, downtown, and I called Sarah and woke her up, I forgot about the three-hour time difference, but I bought her a ticket and she'll fly out here tomorrow."

"Hey, that's great!"

"I even went to the Phone Company and they'll have a phone installed by tomorrow afternoon. Say, while I'm thinking of it, mark this number down, 6472."

"OK, got it, thanks."

"It's amazing how fast we got here and we're almost settled in."

"Right, I get very ticked-off, sometime, about how long it takes for every little thing in the government, but when they want something done ASAP, they move pretty damn fast."

"Yeah, that's for sure."

"You're lucky to have Sarah out here with you, you know it?"

"Of course I do, jerk!"

"Hey, the group of us is going out New Year's eve. It's a Puffy set up and it'll be fun. He says he's been here before and it will be no trouble getting dates."

"Oh yes, he's a hell of a lady's man and he never has any problems finding the lovelies and he's always got an over supply of testosterone."

" Say do you need some help getting the new trigger data and radio references set up in your gear? I'm pretty free now if you need me."

"Nah, thanks Harry, I'll handle this myself and then check it out with the other guys."

"OK. What say we go into town and look around tonight just to get the lay of the land?"

"Sounds good to me. "

"Come on, let's go."

A few moments later Harry and Dick were on their way toward town.

"Dick, maybe we can stop at a market after we take a look at town. I think I want to get some things in the refrigerator so Sarah doesn't have to do it the first thing she gets here."

"Sure, Harry, anytime you say. What's she going to do for a job?"

"Sarah said she would take something temporary like, 'cause we're not supposed to be here too long, right?"

"That's what everyone says. Hey, don't forget, we want to do some digging around here too."

"Of course. I told you that before we left I got some things from the library and took some notes on the area. Let's try to find somebody or a group that's interested and we can get some help."

"Good idea, we should start asking some of the local people about it. Say, when can you get into your new place?"

"They said anytime after six tonight."

"Tell you what, we can walk around a bit, then go get food and stuff and then we can get some dinner. We should get back fairly early; we've got some heavy schedules for the next week or so. I think, once we really get checked out and up to speed, we'll have more time to do some stuff on our own."

"Yep, I'm with you. Hey, Dick, what do you think of the crew?"

"What do ya mean?"

"Well, the guys we've been with, the Navy guys, in general?"

"Spearson basically has a broomstick up his ass and he's a hidden rigid personality—perfect for his Navy job and career. I like him OK, but he puts on a little bit of a front like he's one of the regular guys, but don't dare go against him. Look, I mean, he's friendly, gets us what we want, goes to bat for us most of the time, so I guess we shouldn't complain."

"And what about Dutch? He's been Navy since a little before Pearl Harbor. I didn't know you could stay in the service if you had a limp or some physical problem?"

"Funny you should pick up on that. I asked one of his crew in Philly about that and it seems that Dutch got hit with some shrapnel, mostly in his leg, but he healed up pretty well. Since he was trained as an aircraft mechanic and he became a top notch Chief Mechanic and outfitter, they keep him on. He fakes a good walk when he's near brass. The guy told me that when he's tired his limp is worse, but mostly he covers it up pretty good."

"Hey, stop down on Fremont Street, I want to buy some wine for our first dinner here."

"How 'bout over there, see it, Ethel's liquor store."

"Good, pull over and I'll jump in there. Want anything?"

"Nah, thanks."

Dick pulled past the Las Vegas club and pulled over near

the Pioneer club. Harry ran across the street and returned in a few minutes with a bag which klunked dangerously as he put it on the back floor.

"Hey, watch it, if we get this military limo piece of crap wine-soaked they'll have my ass in a sling. They'll think I was drinking in it."

"OK, OK. It's fine."

"What you get?"

"Just one red and one white, listen, with the airfare and a couple of months down on the apartment, I'm lucky I didn't have to get ginger ale."

Dick headed to the strip and south in the slow lane. They gawked at either side of the road as they passed the Sahara, El Rancho Vegas, the Last Frontier, Desert Inn, the Sands and the Flamingo. They both looked like they were watching a tennis match.

"Wow, these places are magnificent, look at that one, holy smokes!"

"What say we get your groceries and then come back here and go in one and have some dinner."

"OK by me, just promise me we won't lose more than five or ten bucks. I mean, I'm really broke."

"Sure! Hey, did you see the sign on the Sahara? Sugar Ray Robinson will be there next month."

"To do what?

"How the hell do I know, doesn't he dance or something?"

"Who cares. All I know is that Sarah will, absolutely, want to see Frank Sinatra at the Desert Inn as soon as she gets here."

"Terrific, now all we have to do is find a market. I hear that every place has one-arm bandits except the churches."

"That's encouraging. Do we get to see them in the men's rooms next to the urinals?"

"They do say this is the place to piss your money away!"

"You're a funny guy."

"Yeah and my father used to say that his brother left here once with a small fortune—the only trouble was that he got out here with a very large fortune!"

*JANUARY 25, 1953: AMARGOSA DESERT, NEVADA*

Harry sat dozing in the front seat of the military sedan as Dick drove west on a very bumpy, corrugated dirt road. They were approaching the Amargosa River and there they hoped to find a guy named Mickey Haws. They had been told at the bar in Lathrop Wells that if anyone knew about digging it was Mickey. Harry allowed himself to be bounced and rocked into a near coma and with his eyes closed, he thought of the hectic past four weeks. Most of the gear had been calibrated, checked for accuracy and the radiation detection devices were, generally, in place, secure and alarmed. The teams had examined all the data at hand regarding radiation, fallout, on and off-site accumulated doses, hazards of radiation, meteorological trajectories, safety criteria and so many other reports, files and logs that he thought his head would explode.

One thing that ate at him was just below the surface. He couldn't help but wonder about the accuracy of some of the radiation figures, for there seemed to be some ratio discrepancies. He knew he could be in error just on the basis of the huge amount of information they had been wading through. Most of the time he forgot it and relied on the workmanship of the Ph.D. types to keep things up to snuff.

The two of them had been looking forward to this whole day of roaming through the boondocks looking for ideal places to dig and search for artifacts. What little reading about the area had been reviewed, but this was a superficial review, at best, for they were so deluged with work-related reading that the historical and archaeological local information sat on a back burner. They had been out a few times for a few hours at a time. They had investigated the area between Indian Springs and Desert Rock. The area near the town of Mercury was a bust and Cactus Springs yielded a few things down in dry gulches, but they were nothing to crow about. They did find a small cave at Spectre Mountain about three hundred feet up. It was only about four feet high and about seven feet deep and it looked as though it may have been a burial site. It was obvious that it had been searched and ruined by people that didn't care. They were very excited about some primitive scratchings on one of the walls, however. They took a few moments to copy the petroglyphs into their search diaries. One late afternoon the week before, they had ventured further up through Beatty and Scotty's Junction and learned a great deal from locals in the bars, all three of them. It got so late that they found themselves after ten thirty at the Mizpah Hotel in Tonapah. Harry called Sarah to tell her he didn't get kidnapped by a bunch of dangerous cowboys and to inform her that he and Dick were going to spend the night at the hotel and go directly to work the next morning.

This day, typically cold and bitter, they dressed for the freezing winds that they had met on previous treks. The river came into view and what was left of the dirt track stopped abruptly at a mound of boulders about twenty feet short of the river. The boulders looked like some giants, playing at marbles, had piled up their treasures into a pyramidal formation. Across the river and a few thousand feet beyond was, according to the map, the California State line and Death Valley. After taking some fortification in the way of coffee from a large thermos, they got out of the car and walked to the river's edge. On their right and on a bluff about 15 feet above the river they saw the glint of a reflection from an old, small house trailer. It was perched on several small boulders to get it off the ground and smoke floated out of a vent pipe atop the trailer. As they made their way along the river's bank,

"Harry, how the hell you think this Mickey guy got that damn thing up there?"

"Beats me, ask him if he's there."

"Say, look among those trees, is that a truck?"

"Yeah, it looks like an old army jeep with a plywood cover."

"You're right. It looks like he replaced the upper body with wood."

"Smart for out here. Who would want an open jeep out here?"

"Hey, there he is up there."

"Howdy men, I've been waitin' on you two."

"Hi there. How do we get up there?"

"Come around to the rear and you'll see some rock steps I put in there just for you city guys."

"Thanks, and how come you knew we were on our way?"

"My pal Smitty radioed me as soon as you left. He figured that if I didn't see you soon that I should send the Marines for you both. You'd be surprised how many people get lost up here. Why, the count must be up to six in the last ten years!"

"That doesn't seem to be very many in ten years."

"It is when some of them is bringin' you either grub or money."

They reached the top huffing and groaning a bit, attesting to the long hours spent at a desk or in front of some stupid electronic gear instead of having fun and some good exercise. Mickey almost crushed their hand with each shake and invited them into the warmth of his home. His broad sincere smile extended across his well-tanned and lined face. It was not the kind of grin that vanished immediately, for it remained for quite some time attesting to its' earnest origins.

With coffee, and comfortable without their coats in front of an old Ben Franklin style stove, they saw a cozy warm place with a quilt-covered single bed and two chairs. In the back was a small kitchen area and a tiny school desk loaded with specimens, bones, books, rocks and Lord knows what. Out a back window they could see a small hut covered with a few layers of sheet metal over wood rafters and canvas covers at the end they could see. In this setting began a very friendly relationship bound by their mutual love of the dig, the artifact, the history and, most of all, preservation.

### *FEBRUARY 1, 1953: DESERT ROCK, NEVADA*

A few of the guys, Harry and Dick were munching away at sandwiches for lunch after a hectic morning setting up schedules and analysis models to be used during their portion of the shot program. They, all, had responsibilities during the earlier shots as learning and field testing procedures. Most of them were privy to the essentials.

"Listen, there will be several aircraft at the periphery of the cloud on all the blasts. The AEC conducts their own radiation tests. I imagine at some point all the radiation data will be organized and combined so someone, some group, can examine the results closely."

"Yeah, we hope! It'll take 'em ten years to find out what we're doin' here and then they'll find out why we all've been glowin' in the freakin' dark."

"And why we're pissing carbonated water, too!"

"Hey, guys, I'm sure we're safe. They wouldn't have us here if we weren't."

"Right, Dick, sure—sure."

"Hey, last night I read that the drone, the Skyraider, is in use in Korea now as combat planes and the damn plane can carry the exact same bomb load as the B-17 bombers during WWII."

"Hey, that's fascinating! What did you do, run out of girlie magazines?"

"I've been looking at some things this AM and a couple of items jumped out at me. The first time an atom bomb was used in Japan, at Hiroshima, it was called 'little boy'. The thing had a 10-ton kiloton yield and the next one at Nagasaki was called 'fatman' and was a 20-kt job."

"Yeah, so?"

"Well, here we are sitting in the middle of so-called atomic experiments and if you look at the shot info, we're involved with kt's of anywhere from point 2 on up to, get this, the 'Simon' blast is supposed to be 43 kt's."

"Jesus!"

"Harry, what are you frowning about?"

"I'm still worried about what I'm sure are serious errors in the radiation levels. I've written a formal report about the levels to the brass, but they say that I'm incorrect and I'm over reacting, but they would look into it and get back to me."

"Have they?"

"No, and I don't really expect them to, either."

## *FEBRUARY 2, 1953: AMARGOSA DESERT, NEVADA*

Over the next few months Dick and Harry spent whatever free time they had with Mickey, searching, digging and mostly learning. Haws had told them that he grew up in Blue Jay, a very small place east on route 6 out of Tonopah. His mother busied herself raising seven kids and his father was a carpenter and woodworker. In fact, his dad had made the old bench which sat on the high sidewalk at the Mizpah Hotel, the one where the same two Indians were perched most of the time. Mickey was taught the local lore by his dad and the local Indians, many who helped out with his father's work when he had a big job to do. A big job in those days was anything that was over one day. Mickey, with ease, told the guys that at the end of the war, after being in the Philippines, Corregidor, several

Japanese prison camps, a prison ship to the mainland of Japan and two years of forced labor, came out of the Army, in his words, "diseased, deranged, demented and basically fucked-up." Hospitals, medication and eventually a VA disability check each month that saw him through what few needs he had.

Haws led the guys through a great deal of the area and even sneaked into the restricted fringes of the government test ranges. They observed and made digs in irregular surface structures, many dry lakes that were plentiful in the southwest of the state. Everything fascinated them; strange rock layers, Indian artifacts, old animal bones, the ghost town of Rhyolite where they dug into an old abandoned privy and found some real neat bottles. One of the small bottles was a medicine bottle embossed 'Dr. Leon's Infant Syrup*Ziegler & Smith*PHILA'. Mickey informed them that patent medicine bottles probably came out this way via wagons and later medicine 'drummers' would sell them from town to town. Bottles and other items that could be sold for some extra cash is how Mickey added to his pension. Harry and Dick made notes and drew simple drawings of what they saw and found, leaving anything to be sold by Mickey. They also helped out by buying all the meals and any food and sodas they would bring on their treks. Harry, particularly, would make sure that he overbought so as to have much in the way of leftovers for Mickey.

Other jaunts, led by Haws, took them to the west a bit, into Death Valley. Going over Daylight Pass at sunup was a sight to see; it even forced a smile and a 'wow' out of Dick. They spent several of their trips in the Valley, climbing around in the Funeral Mountains which turned out to be a nice source of several fossils.

Harry would miss about every third or fourth trip, for he wanted to spend time with Sarah when she was off from work. At those times, Dick and Mickey would go out together and when the weather started to warm up, Dick would commandeer a jeep and with that they could scamper into more of the rougher areas.

### FEBRUARY 26, 1953: LAS VEGAS, NEVADA

Harry and Dick were drinking from their beer bottles in Harry's kitchen. Sarah was at work, on the day shift, and Harry had volunteered to do dinner for the three of them. As Harry was stirring a concoction of chopped tomatoes, hamburger meat, garlic, dried basil and oregano, Dick was setting the small kitchen table. Harry threw into the pot a small handful of pine nuts and, as Dick watched with a look of surprise, Harry poured into the pot a small cup of black coffee.

"What the hell are you doing?"

"Huh?"

"What's the coffee for? I've never seen anybody do that before."

"Well, now you have."

"Yeah, but what for?

"Listen, my mom's aunt was a fantastic cook and she taught my mom to add a cup of black coffee to a pot of spaghetti gravy."

"Listen, I like cream and sugar in my coffee, are you going to add that too?"

"No, I don't think so."

"But why the coffee, seriously?"

"It's supposed to add body to the sauce, that's all."

"Whatever you say, friend, you're the chef tonight."

"Say, start washing the lettuce and other stuff for the salad will you, please? And cut it up and there's wine vinegar and oil in that cabinet over there and you can make the salad dressing, OK?"

"Sure thing, and I suppose I can stick a broom up my ass and sweep the floor while I'm doing all that, right?"

"I'm sure you can handle it, hell, you're a college graduate."

"OK, here I go. Where are your salad plates?"

"While you're doing that, listen, I've been rechecking the logbooks and radiation reports for the detonations prior to our arrival, you know, the data on previous test shots. I've made some comparison charts of those data and the radiation expectation figures for our tests and they're way off."

"How do you mean?"

"Well, the expected levels from operation Upshot-Knothole are well below the actual levels already on the books as factual. I've been concerned that radiation effects will be a hell of a lot greater than expected and everyone will be overexposed and maybe hurt."

"Harry, we've been over this a dozen times. I've seen those reports and there's so much variation and differences in the reports that I think it's impossible to make those assumptions. Anyway, you've always been over-sensitive about such things. Listen, I mentioned before that the guys running these things would not put us in jeopardy, right?"

"Ugh, well, I guess not. But it just doesn't seem as solid as I would like it to be."

"See? That's the cautious Harry we all love and cherish."

"OK, OK, I get it. I'll try to be a bit more positive, OK? I'd still like to hear back from the brass, though."

"Good! Listen, I'm almost done here, you going to put the spaghetti into the water yet? It's about to boil over."

"Yep! Sarah should be home any minute. You put the salads on the table and I'll cut the bread. We'll be ready to eat in about fifteen minutes."

"Hey, that's good. Say, where's the grated cheese?"

*DECEMBER 2, 1992: ATLANTIC CITY EXPRESSWAY,*

*NEW JERSEY*

Oz, tan and wearing sunglasses, was cruising toward Atlantic City at a steady 65 miles an hour with Max beside him in the passenger seat. Max was singing along with the radio, trying to remember the words to 'Darn That Dream'.

"Max, you never know all the words to any song. What's with that?"

"Who knows? I can remember a thousand jokes but, you're right, I do a lot of la-la-la-ing when I sing. Hey, you turned the radio off, am I that bad?"

"No, no, not that. Listen, I've been thinking about the Harry Connors thing."

"Yeah, so?"

"Well, we've got some of the invitations and info in the mail and all we have to do is wait on the responses and I've put up all the shelves I have to in the house—"

"Hell, you've bought enough shelving to do my house too!"

"Yeah, OK, listen will ya? I'm very intrigued by this disappearance thing. I got on the Internet this week and I found reams of stuff on Nevada and Desert Rock and I printed out a bunch of pages on Operation Upshot-Knothole. This was the name of the atomic tests out there that Tishman told me about."

"Oh, yeah, the time that Harry and Dick were out there together?"

"Right, that's it. Tishman is no great source of information; he's always been closed like a clam. You remember, always the pal and loud sometimes, but when you really think back on him, he was never humanly friendly and giving of himself like Harry was."

"I do remember, yep, that's right on."

"Anyway, I read the stuff over, and I have the printout in the trunk for you, and I get an idea to find out what happened to Harry's wife. I make a few calls and finally wind up with Phil Marsh again and he told me that Sarah is in State College and has been there for years running a business with a friend and she went back to her maiden name. He even knew that her son's name is Adam and he works in Philly."

"What's her maiden name?"

"It's Kirkendahl. So, I didn't want to disturb her unless I had to and I looked in the white pages and there's only one listing. I think it's got to be Adam."

"I take it you didn't call."

"I wanted to run this past you first. What do you think? Do you think we'll open up a bag of worms by prying into this?"

"I don't know, but you have me curious now. What could hurt? You could call and the worse could happen he could tell you to get lost or he could be a friendly type and we could go see him."

"Good, that's what I'll do."

Oz was approaching an exit and as he rounded the exit ramp curve,

"Maxie, sport, you going to shoot some craps with me?"

"You know me, Oz, I'll watch for a while then I'll walk on the boards and meet you later."

" Let's head for the 'White House' first and split one of their subs, OK?"

"Sounds good to me. I can do the dice and taste the onions all afternoon. What could be bad?"

# PART 3

# THE INVESTIGATION

Puffy was in his office gathering his notes, and at the same time, speaking on the phone to the Commanding General, Desert Rock.

"I don't know where the drone is, General. I've been talking to the tower here, Las Vegas, and the people at Desert Rock, and everyone comes up blind."

"Commander, my folks here have checked by radio and phone, in every direction, and no sightings have been reported. I've got half a squadron going through our 'downed aircraft emergency procedures'. You get to your debriefing and get whatever information you can from your teams."

"Yes, Sir, will do . . ."

"And Commander, make sure everything is on tape. I'm sending Colonel Pennington, the Director of Weapon Effects Tests, to your 1400 meeting and I want him to coordinate the final report."

"Yes, Sir, I'll speak to you later."

Puffy returned the phone to its cradle and noticed that his hand was sweaty. He couldn't believe that the damn thing was nowhere, no-place. He shook his head as if it would help, grabbed his folders, and walked to the debriefing room.

The debriefing was always scheduled an hour after the operation was completed.

It was the first of two debriefings. The early meeting reviewed all pertinent action and data results from all sources and quickly reviewed the entire process. Suggestions were formulated regarding the corrections and or additions needed to improve efficiency and the overall adequacy of the procedures. Everyone concerned, from the top brass to the ground crews, knew that everything they were doing was from scratch. They were groundbreakers, for none of the things they were doing was ever done before. Improvements were important and absolutely mandatory if their program was to succeed.

As he entered the room, he saw a group of VX-4 pilots all chattering at once. They all looked tired and wired; a common air of concern creased their faces. Puffy stormed into the room, almost knocking down two of the techs getting coffee at a table near the door.

Someone yelled, "attention on deck" and the chattering ceased. As he took his seat at the head of a large rectangular table, he boomed,

"Everyone sit the hell down!"

As the chairs filled up, Tishman came into the room, nodded to a few of the men and took a seat.

"Tishman, where the hell is Harry?"

"How the hell do I know? I looked all over this freakin' place—I just don't know."

"Before we begin this debriefing; I want to make a statement. As you are all probably aware, and I say this with a great deal of concern, Harry Connors has been missing for about thirteen hours, and I had to formally notify Base Security of the facts."

Without a pause, he turned on the tape recorder situated in front of him and continued.

"Gentlemen, the time is now 0800 on April 18, 1953. Lcdr. Spearson is the debriefing officer. The purpose of this debriefing is to determine, to the best of our abilities, the events leading up to the loss of the drone, and to assess the data to determine the cause.

OK, let's begin with Preflight. Lt. Kelly, you taxied the bird into position. Report."

"The preflight was nominal, all systems checked out OK, including the radio control. I taxied into position on the runway, made my final checks coordinating with you, left the aircraft, returned to the van."

"Chief Mitchell, you're next."

"I followed Lt. Peterson in the van, and when he climbed out of the cockpit, I prepared to strap the dummy in. After its installation, I followed procedures for checking the continuity of the circuitry, which went off without a hitch, and I returned to the van."

Spearson looked at Tishman;

"You're on, Mr. Tishman."

"About midnight, I was in my office and got a call from one of our techs that some of our receptors were malfunctioning. I got a hold of Harry and asked him to check into it. He said he was leaving right away. When I got to the van this morning, and started to check out my gear, indications were that the instrumentation on the dummy was not fully working, and that's when I asked you to abort the mission."

Spearson looked out sharply,

"I'll repeat myself for the record, Dick. ' Go,No-Go' criteria states that since there are a limited number of operations scheduled, the primary goal of this program is to assess blast damage on the drone. Your mission, which I agree is very important, is secondary. In addition to that, all your other instrumentation was working and, based on those facts, I gave the order to go."

Tishman continued,

"As I stated previously, at H-hour, I lost all signals; all the drone telemetering data ceased; and after checking the van equipment and verifying that it was functioning properly, I

83

can only conclude that damage to the drone was so severe that all my equipment was destroyed."

Spearson continued,

"I had the same thing happen to my equipment at the "FOX" station and I concur with your conclusion. Lt. Foley, give us your observations."

"Well, I was flying in CHARLIE ONE and as we were getting close to H-hour, I checked visually on Shoshone and Yucca Peaks as I usually do, and I figured that our flight path was too far southwest and closer to ground zero than our flight plan called for. I radioed you with my concerns and was very happy to hear you order us out, throttle to the wall. After the blast, we were being tossed around quite a bit and visibility was poor and I lost sight of the bird. Both CHARLIE TWO and I think we saw debris northwest of our flight path but we can't be sure. There may have been a more dense accumulation of debris at some point, and we marked it on our charts."

Puffy noted that the reported coordinates were relatively the same, but he knew that each of the chase planes was observing from slightly different altitudes, airspeed and directions.

Foley continued,

"That's when we returned to home base. I am positive we were off course at H-hour."

Spearson responded,

"That's real interesting: if you will all look at my radar plot (Chief Mitchell unrolled the map showing the radar plot superimposed on the flight plan), you will see that the bird was right on course, right down the center of the prescribed path. Dutch, when did we last calibrate?"

"Two days ago, sir."

Spearson continued,

"Well, we better run a check right away."

"Peterson, put the beacon in CHARLIE TWO, get

airborne, and coordinate the calibration with Dutch. When we run the test, I want a Base Air Force type monitoring as an impartial observer. I want the test results yesterday. Let's move it. Tishman, stay a minute."

Everyone got to their feet, and the multiple conversations buzzed and bounced off the bare hard walls of the room like a motor starting.

Tishman sat down across from Puffy, who was still at his desk rewinding the tape. As the two seven-inch reels rotated quickly, Puffy was reminded that he hadn't been on his Harley for months. Hell, the thing was at Pt. Mugu anyway!

He quickly shook this notion and turned to Dick.

"Where the hell is he?"

"Christ, I don't know."

"When was the last time you saw or spoke to him?"

"I told you, we spoke on the phone and he was on his way over here to do a last check on the receptors. We agreed to meet at my desk or the van."

"How did he seem? I mean, OK and all?"

"He seemed fine, I guess."

"What do ya mean, "I guess?"

"I think for a few days he was like a bit edgy and nosy about some of the charts and specs I had on my desk."

"What 'stuff' and how do you mean 'nosy'?"

"Well, some of the new radio-controlled trigger mechanism changes that I was checking out. But listen, Puff, we were all curious—he, maybe, was just interested—you know."

"Well, I'm sure we will all be questioned so be sure to mention some of his 'curiosity', OK?"

\* \* \* \* \* \*

At 0925 Lt. Byron Peterson lifted the F4D Skyray smoothly in the air and climbed to 10,000 feet. He radioed Dutch Mitchell sitting at the FOX station that he was at 'Angels 10' and was ready to proceed. The test was simple enough. Peterson would fly at a constant altitude over precisely known landmarks while Mitchell checked Peterson's verbal "MARK". He then adjusted his pen position to correspond with Peterson's visual "MARKS." Several runs were needed to complete the test. When they were finished, Mitchell took the plot to Cdr. Spearson.

"Commander, it looks like Lt. Foley was correct, the initial run of the test showed the radar plot off by 1700 feet to the southwest."

"How the fuck could that happen, Chief?"

"Sir, I can't say for sure, but it's too great a difference to be normal drift. Either someone accidentally or purposely screwed with the pen potentiometers."

"Chief, are you saying sabotage?"

"No, sir, I just don't know how we could be off that much."

"Thanks, Chief, and from now on we calibrate prior to every mission."

"Yes, Sir, I'll take care of it."

Mitchell saluted and left Spearson's office, leaving him thinking about what he was going to put in his report.

Spearson's final debriefing took place at 1400 hours. Attending the meeting were, all VX-4 and Sandia personnel; Air Force Major Bucky Ward, USAF, who observed the calibration test; Sgt. Ben Weisman, USAF, who had independently monitored the drone flight and calibration test on the Base Tower Radar; and Colonel Sam Pennington, USAF, the Director of Weapon Effects Tests. After three hours of revue and discussions, which were at some times heated, they agreed to send the following communiqué to the Commanding General, Desert Rock.

THE DESTRUCTION OF NAVY DRONE AD SKYRAIDER SERIAL NO.122225, WAS CAUSED BY THE AIRCRAFT BEING OUT OF POSITION AT H-HOUR. BEST ESTIMATES ARE THAT THE AIRCRAFT WAS

APPROXIMATELY 1700 FEET CLOSER TO GROUND ZERO THAN PLANNED, AND THIS CAUSED THE AIRCRAFT STRUCTURE TO BE SUBJECTED TO EXCESSIVE STRESS FROM THE HEAT AND PRESSURE OF THE DETONATION IN EXCESS OF STRUCTURAL DESIGN PARAMETERS. VERIFICATION OF THE STRUCTURAL FAILURE CAN NOT BE COMPLETED UNTIL AIRCRAFT PARTS ARE RECOVERED. TO THIS END, SEARCHES OF THE AREA CONTINUE FOR DEBRIS.

WITH RESPECT TO THE CAUSE OF THE AIRCRAFT BEING OUT OF POSITION, WE CONCLUDE WITH THE FOLLOWING:

1. RADAR PLOTS OF THE MISSION INDICATE THAT THE RADIO CONTROL OF THE AIRCRAFT WAS TEXTBOOK PERFECT AND ALL NAVY OPERATIONAL PERSONNEL PERFORMED THEIR DUTIES IN AN EXEMPLARY MANNER. PERSONNEL AT THE TIME OF THE MISSION COULD NOT HAVE KNOWN THAT THE RADAR EQUIPMENT WAS CALIBRATED INCORRECTLY.

2. SUBSEQUENT TESTS AFTER THE MISSION BY BOTH USN AND USAF PERSONNEL VERIFY THE FACT THAT THE POSITIONAL ERROR OF 1700 FEET WAS CAUSED BY THE PLOTTING EQUIPMENT BEING OUT OF CALIBRATION.

3. ALTHOUGH THE EQUIPMENT WAS CALIBRATED CORRECTLY TWO DAYS EARLIER, PROCEDURES HAVE BEEN MODIFIED TO RUN A CALIBRATION CHECK THE DAY OF ANY PLANNED MISSION.

SPECIAL RECOGNITION IS GIVEN TO LT. BERTRAM FOLEY, USNR, FOR HIS EXCEPTIONAL SKILL IN DETERMINING THAT THE DRONE AIRCRAFT AND CHASE PLANES

WERE IN EXTREMIS, AND REPORTING THIS TO HIS SUPERIORS IN A TIMELY FASHION, THUS SAVING THE LIVES OF HIS WINGMAN AND HIMSELF, IN ADDITION TO PROVIDING FOR THE SAFE RETURN OF THE AIRCRAFT THEY WERE FLYING.

FINALLY, SINCE NO CONCLUSION CAN BE DRAWN AT THIS TIME AS TO THE CAUSE OF THE EQUIPMENT NOT BEING CALIBRATED PROPERLY, AND IN ADDITION TO THE SUDDEN DISAPPEARANCE OF A HIGHLY PLACED SCIEN-TIST ON THIS PROJECT, IT IS RECOMMENDED THAT THE INVESTIGATION BE CONTINUED UNDER THE AUTHORITY OF AIR FORCE AND NAVAL INTELLIGENCE AND ANY OTHER GOV-ERNMENTAL ENTITIES THEY DEEM NECES-SARY. It was signed by the Director of Weapon Effects Tests.

*APRIL 18, 1953: INDIAN SPRINGS AFB, NEVADA*

Dick Tishman left the debriefing feeling somewhat guilty. He had purposely withheld information so that he could in-form his bosses at Sandia first. After all, they paid his salary and, more importantly, the information was proprietary. When he got to his office, he again, very meticulously, rummaged through his desk drawers, files and bookshelves. He then made the same thorough examination of Harry Connors' desk and files. When his examination was complete, he placed a call to Jim Falconer, his supervisor at Sandia headquarters in New Mexico. He suddenly realized that it was after working hours, hung up, and called him at his home.

"Jim, Dick Tishman. Sorry to bother you at home."

"No sweat, Dick. I hear you guys lost the drone . . . did we lose much equipment?"

"I don't think you're going to concern yourself with that, after what I'm about to tell you."

"Sounds like trouble. What?"

"Harry Connors has been missing for about 12 hours. I spoke to him shortly after midnight, and no one has seen him since. He never showed for the operation. I spoke to his wife, trying not to upset her but, without asking her outright, I gathered she still thinks he's on the job. The detachment commander of VX-4 has notified Base Security. More important, the military is turning the investigation over to Air Force and Naval Intelligence."

"Jesus . . . what the hell is going on?"

"The drone was lost because some critical gear was miscalibrated and with Harry missing, they're calling in the big guns. There's more, Jim. I've searched and searched and I'm positive that some rough spec notes and drawings of the changes I've proposed for the new remote trigger mechanism are gone. I have the originals but the rough copies are missing. At this point, you're the only one I've told."

"Do you think they were stolen? Can't they be misplaced somewhere?"

"I don't believe so, Jim . . . and that's not the whole story . . ."

"I'll bet, when things go wrong, there is unfortunately always more. Tell me the rest."

"Well, I really feel hesitant about saying this, but under the circumstances, I feel I must. Harry's been nosing around my desk for the last few weeks asking questions and more than once, I caught him reading some of the reports and looking at the drawings, for which he doesn't have a "need to know." He's always been a curious guy, and he does have clearance, but with things as they are, I thought I had better mention it to you."

"You did the right thing, Dick . . . you said no one knows about the missing paperwork?"

"That's correct, Jim, no one but you."

"Good, keep it that way for now. I'm going to get a hold of Bob Stringer, our Head of Security, and have him follow through. I'll make sure he contacts you first thing in the morning . . . This is really terrible, I can't believe Harry is involved, he's a good guy!"

"Neither can I. I'm sorry I had to bring it up, but you know . . . under the circumstances."

"I know how difficult that was for you. You guys knew each other since college, right?"

"That's right, we were like brothers. I was best man at his wedding."

"Thanks for calling, Dick. Hold tight until Stringer gets back to you."

*APRIL 24, 1953: INDIAN SPRINGS AFB, NEVADA*

Frantic would be an understatement in describing the activities that went on during the next few days. After Bob Stringer had informed authorities of the missing documents, the FBI had been called in, and the investigation was being handled as a possible espionage case. All project personnel had been questioned numerous times, as is the case when several governmental agencies were involved. Each agency had their own turf to protect, and so the interviews were tailored to meet their own needs. Harry Connors' house had been searched, many articles were removed, and authorities continued to return to insure that nothing had been missed. Sarah had been interviewed several times and was near collapse from emotional exhaustion. She was fortunate to have the Mifflins as neighbors. They were sympathetic to her situation, and provided whatever comfort they could. There was no sympathy shown by the investigating agencies as they continued their search for evidence. Dick Tishman tried several times to call Sarah without success. He stopped trying as he came to realize more and more that it was his suspicions that had focused the guilt on Harry.

Martin Haskell, agent-in-charge of the Las Vegas field office of the FBI, and the man now in charge of the overall investigation, held his first formal meeting with the senior group of individuals composing his task force. The task force consisted of high-ranking members of both Naval and Air Force Intelligence sent from Washington, the security chiefs of both Camp Desert Rock and Indian Springs AFB, Bob Stringer from Sandia, and Haskell's own staff out of Las Vegas. The job of coordinating the activities of the various groups that the task members represented was consuming more of Haskell's time than he was able to spend on the actual investigation. He had never been confronted with such an overwhelming and cumbersome task. To resolve this problem, he had requested and had been granted the use of the services of Tom Chapman, a young veteran investigator out of Washington, whom he knew and respected. Tom was given the assignment of gathering and sifting through all the evidence that was being collected, and preparing progress reports for the task force members. This left Haskell time to deal with the politics of the situation. After opening the meeting, Haskell turned to Tom Chapman to lay before the task force all the information that was verified to be correct, ignoring for the moment speculative theories. He did so in a precise, perfunctory manner.

"Gentlemen, the report follows:

1. Harry Connor's car was found intact, parked in the area reserved for project personnel.
2. Fingerprints found in the car belonged to Connors, his wife Sarah, and his co-worker, Dick Tishman.
3. Nothing out of the ordinary was found in the car other than a torn piece of paper, which is being analyzed to see if the source can be determined.
4. The gate sentry log indicated that Connors had entered

the base at 0106 hours on April 18, 1953. There was no log entry showing him leaving the base.

5. After reviewing the tapes of all of the interviews to date, apparently the only person outside of family and project personnel that Connors had any routine contact with was Mickey Haws. Both Dick Tishman and Sarah Connors had disclosed this information. A FBI agent has been dispatched to interview him.

6. Tishman had reported that the last time he had seen the missing documents was early in the morning, just past midnight, on April 18. The documents had not been secured properly as prescribed in the SECDEF DIRECTIVE NAV445789. Tishman also reported seeing Connors going through his papers and drawings on at least two occasions.

7. Sandia officials have verified that the missing documents, code name 'Helen' are classified TOP SECRET and NEED TO KNOW ONLY, and their loss is a serious breach of security. Washington believes that the Soviets could advance, by years, their ability to detonate their first H-bomb, if the information were to get in their hands.

8. An ongoing FBI undercover operation, photographing people going in and out of a suspected Soviet drop site in downtown Las Vegas, produced photos showing a man dressed in similar attire as Harry Conners and with the same general physical appearance. The report also indicated that a shorter, stockier man was seen talking briefly to the taller man. Additional analysis is ongoing, to try to determine the identity of the observed men. The report ended with the note that the heavier man was observed leaving the site, but the taller man was not seen leaving.

9. Some small debris, thought to be that of the drone, was recovered and has been sent to the FBI lab in Washington for analysis. They are working around the clock to get us the results ASAP.

10. Our major effort continues to be the search for Connors. Local law enforcement agencies have been contacted and are helping in the search. All the standard procedures for a nationwide missing-person manhunt have been activated. We've placed particular emphasis on the known Soviet egress routes via Mexico and Canada. To date, we have no sightings.

Please continue to have your people coordinate with me, so there is only one source cataloguing all the evidence."

Prior to adjourning the meeting, Haskell addressed the members of the task force.

"Gentlemen, I can not emphasize strongly enough our need to keep this investigation under tight security and make it look to the outside that this is a missing person investigation. If this is indeed a Soviet operation, then we would like them to get comfortable in their knowledge that we are completely unaware of it. This will give us an advantage in the possible discovery of other evidence if they don't go underground. In addition to that, there is a political necessity. Washington has informed me that Senator Joseph McCarthy is attempting to get support in the Senate to start a congressional investigation of Soviet influence in our government. I'm sure I don't have to elaborate on what that can mean to us all if he gets a hold of this mess and decides to start here."

Over the next few days, the investigation produced the following:

· The FBI lab report dealing with the examination of the debris determined, with the help of Douglas Aircraft engineers, that it was from the AD Skyraider. Tests also revealed that there had been structural failure due to excessive heat and pressure.

· The most startling piece of evidence was the discovery that the torn piece of paper found in Harry Connors' car matched perfectly the partially torn cover sheet on Dick Tishman's original trigger-mechanism documents.

- Analysis of the photographs taken was inconclusive in the positive identification of Connors as the person entering the suspected drop site. Although the general build matched that of Connors, it also matched several other project members. The Identity of the shorter, heavier man was inconclusive, as well.

- It was the unanimous conviction of the task force that Harry Connors had stolen the documents and that he had successfully eluded capture. They also concluded that he was no longer in the United States and that very little more would be forthcoming. There was little evidence to bring charges of espionage against Connors in absentia, nor was the political climate conducive to doing so.

Although the suspected Soviet drop site in Las Vegas was continuously under observation, no new clues pertaining to the present case were ever found.

On June 4, the final operation of UPSHOT-KNOTHOLE took place. It was code named CLIMAX and consisted of an airdrop by a B-36 bomber over the test site with a yield of 61 kilotons, three times that of the bomb dropped on Nagasaki.

Shortly thereafter, Commander Puffy Spearson took his VX-4 detachment back to their home base at Pt. Mugu, California.

Dick Tishman took his team and equipment back to Sandia, in Albuquerque. After the project personnel dispersed to their various locations, Martin Haskell returned to his office in Las Vegas and left Tom Chapman the job of closing down the task force.

Chapman went through the evidence one more time before packing it away. Something kept bothering him but he couldn't put his finger on it. As Chapman reviewed the evidence, he thought about the questions that were still unanswered. Harry's background check showed nothing that was suspicious. He was not a loner, was well liked by his fellow workers . . . more so than Tishman. Sarah had agreed to take a lie detector test, and even though it was not that reliable, the indications were that she knew nothing about the theft or Harry's disappearance. He believed Sarah was telling the truth. They were recently married and by all accounts, extremely happy and very close. Why wouldn't he plan to meet her or take her with him? Why was she completely in the dark? Harry must have been one hell of an actor. A check of their financial situation showed no large balances or any questionable deposits. Of course this didn't mean anything, they could have been hidden. Yet . . . was Harry working alone? If not, it couldn't have been project personnel, their whereabouts had been confirmed. It was certainly possible to get off the base without a car and not be seen. But then what, picked up? No sightings. It was just too clean. What about Tishman? The men didn't like him and neither did Chapman. He was a little too arrogant for his liking. He had checked his background and one of the things out of the ordinary was that he had spent his sophomore year at the Sorbonne in Paris. Not that there was anything wrong with that, just different. He also was a member of a student radical group at Penn State but he had reviewed the investigation for his clearance at Sandia, and nothing was awry, just college kid stuff. Still puzzled, he closed the evidence box.

The next day, Chapman returned to Washington with all of the evidence and remained in charge of the case.

95

# PART 4

# ADAM

*MAY 3, 1953: LAS VEGAS, NEVADA*

Sarah had been terrible and terrified for the few weeks after Harry's disappearance. She had no local support to speak of, and she didn't have any family anywhere. Her folks had died several years before and there were no siblings to call on. One aged aunt remained in the small town in Pennsylvania where Sarah was born and raised. The aunt was in her eighties and in a Catholic senior's residence in Old Forge and Sarah could not and would not burden the old woman.

Dumbfounded by the mere thought of Harry's dishonesty and the subterfuge of which he was accused, Sarah was either sobbing without apparent letup or she found herself in a near catatonic state, late at night, alone and afraid. Some days she was so down that it was late in the evening before she realized that she had not eaten anything all day or had anything to drink. Very often, she was still in her pajamas in the middle of the afternoon. A couple of girls from work stopped in a few times and the wives of two of Harry's colleagues had called, asking if they could help in some way. Her embarrassment forced her to reject help at a time when she desperately needed it. In the short time that she and Harry had been in Las Vegas, they didn't have much time to develop close friends. To add to her plight, she feared that she'd picked up some form of flu. She was constantly in the bathroom, either peeing a lot or throwing up. At first, she felt that it was her constant anxiety, lack of sleep and no food of any account.

Her downstairs neighbors, the Mifflins, an older retired

couple, tried to be helpful by offering some hot broth and some cold chicken one evening. When they went up the one flight to see her, it was immediately apparent that she had lost some weight and, in Mr. Mifflin's words,

"Hell, girl, you look like death warmed over!"

"I can't seem to work up an appetite for anything."

"Well, first thing in the morning, the Mrs. and I are taking you to our doctor. He's only about ten minutes from here. And if you don't come with us, I'm going to dump you into the pickup and take you anyway! Hear me?"

"OK, yes . . . thank you."

At 10:10 the following morning, Sarah sat in Dr. Stone's office after he had completed his examination and questions. The Mifflins, like security guards, sat in the waiting room waiting for their charge.

"I've taken some blood, as you know, and some other tests will be done on the samples I took. Sarah, when I asked, you mentioned that you had missed one period."

"That's not rare with me. In the past, when I get sick or nervous about something—I've missed some before."

"Well, I won't know anything for a hundred percent for awhile, but I can make fairly good guesses, because I've been doing this for 37 years."

"What guesses?"

"I think, number one, that you have a mild bladder infection and . . . number two, and more important, I think that you might be pregnant."

"Oh, God!"

Sarah had mixed feelings about the news, but mostly she felt numb all over. Among the many things she worried about, one of the main things had to do with how she was going to care for herself and now with this possibility, she would have to take care of a baby, too. Knowing that she lacked Harry's presence beside her and helping her and . . .

"Oh shit!"

The Mifflins were very supportive and Sarah, finally, allowed them to help.

Dr. Stone's guesses had been right. Six days of some new, mild antibiotic chased the bladder thing away and he had given her some medication and vitamins to increase her appetite and build her up. The neighbors, always extremely attentive, even took her to their priest. They met twice a week for a time and Sarah came to realize that the uncertainty of Harry's whereabouts, her now being alone in the world, the guilt she felt, were all valid reasons for her state of mind. After a bit, she came to understand that the guilt she felt was misplaced and even now, from the moment of the accusations until now, she knew, absolutely, that Harry had done nothing wrong. Harry was either sick or something bad had happened to him. She prayed that he was alive and would return to her.

One close friend, with whom Sarah had kept in touch, Peggy Kintner, lived and worked in State College, Pennsylvania. Peg had gotten a job there after graduation and stayed on. Sarah had spent the best four years of her life there and it dawned on her that she could live there and be close to her friend. A college town was always a great place to get a job. Certainly she could get something better than waitressing, as far as salary goes. Peg was the administrative assistant to a real estate and land developer in Centre County.

Sarah had written and called Peggy several times since Harry disappeared, so she knew a little of the circumstances. When Sarah phoned and told her of her plan to join her at Penn State, Peg was thrilled. They had been Sorority sisters and roommates, first in Atherton Hall, then Simmons Hall. Peg was still single and liked very much the notion of a close friend being even closer.

*MAY 6, 1953: LAS VEGAS, NEVADA*

Dick Tishman had been very busy these last few weeks. He had spent much time on the phone with his Sandia superiors, written a dozen reports, spent innumerable hours with several investigators and as many hours collecting and sorting his data from the last shots. He had been instructed, as were others, not to discuss the present situation with anyone not directly involved with the investigation. He had attempted, at least five or six times, to reach Sarah. He had gotten no response at the apartment and one call to her workplace proved unfruitful, for he was told that she had quit.

At around quarter past six PM he was parking his government car a half block from Sarah's place. He admitted to himself that he was a bit anxious about seeing her and half hoping that she would not be in. He did want to see her, but he really hadn't the slightest idea what to say to her. Two seconds after his knock, Sarah opened the door, turned, left the door ajar without a word, and walked back into the kitchen. Dick, hesitantly, stepped inside, closed the door quietly and followed her. She was sitting at the table holding a mug of what looked like tea in both hands, head down and sobbing gently.

"I'm awful sorry, Sarah. I tried and tried to get you on the phone and I wasn't even allowed to see anyone for a couple of weeks. I wanted you to know that I was sorry and could I do something. Hell, you know that you and Harry and me, we're friends."

"I know, Dick. They told me several times that no one at the base except them could speak to me for a while and never about what happened. Is there anything that you're allowed to tell me?"

Dick saw in Sarah's face unfamiliar lines, deep-set darkened eyes, a much thinner face, almost gaunt-like, and a dull pallor that frightened him.

"There's nothing to tell you. And if there was something, even though I'm not supposed to say anything, I would tell you if I knew anything."

"I'm leaving here as soon as I can. I'm sick of people coming and asking the same damn questions over and over. I told them I'm going back to Pennsylvania."

"You are? When do you think?"

"Soon. I've been talking to Peggy, my old roommate, and she wants me to go and stay with her."

"Hey I think that's a super idea. What will you do there?"

"You mean, besides having a baby!"

"What? Oh, wow, are you kidding?"

"Yes, sure, I've just been in the mood to make jokes."

"Oh, Jeez! Are you OK with money and everything?"

"Yes, I'm OK. We have some money here at the bank and I still have our savings account at that Liberty Bank at Broad and Arch in Philadelphia."

"I'll be leaving here soon, too. I'm not supposed to say anything to anyone so please keep it to yourself."

"Sure. Where are you going?"

"Our, I mean, my boss at Sandia has ordered me back to New Mexico; they don't seem to want me here and in the middle of things. They'll send out some new people to carry on with the stuff here and I'm supposed to work on some connected projects. I don't know. I'm tired of all this, anyway. It seems that the past few weeks have taken all the steam out of me."

"I know exactly what you're talking about. You want some tea or something?"

"No. No, thanks. How 'bout coming out and having some supper with me? You know, nothing fancy, just something simple. It looks like you could use some food."

"Thanks, no, Dick. I haven't felt like eating much of anything. You go ahead."

---

"Listen, I'll not be leaving for a little while and if you need me or anything, please call me at the Base. I'll get my new address and phone number at Sandia to you before you leave and we'll stay in touch. I'll even come to State College and visit. Would that be OK?"

"Absolutely, sure."

"I wouldn't mind meeting up with Peg again, too. Is she still single?"

"Yes, she is. And Dick, thanks for coming by. Why don't you call again before you leave and maybe I'll take you up on your supper offer? Maybe there will be some news. Please call me if you hear anything."

"Of course I will."

Dick climbed out of his chair, pushed it back under the table, leaned over and pecked Sarah's cheek. Without saying anything else, they walked to the front door, smiled and with a wave, Dick was outside and down the steps. He looked back up and Sarah, with a weak smile, waved and shut the door.

Dick never called, and a few days before Sarah left town, she called the base wanting to say goodbye to him. She was told by one of the techs that knew who she was, that Tishman had returned to New Mexico the week before.

*JUNE 1, 1953: LAS VEGAS, NEVADA*

Sarah was leaving today. The prospect of moving out of Las Vegas with all its memories and reminders, lightened her mood a little bit. Living in a small town like State College pleased her, for there was a place that had only happy memories. Staying with one of her few friends would be good for her. Sarah had thought that a small friendly town was just right, for a large city, like Philadelphia, for her, would be cold and lonesome and she feared that she would get lost in such a huge place.

The Mifflins were, literally, lifesavers. With their support she had gained some weight, looked healthier and Dr. Stone had assured her that she would have no problems with her pregnancy. He urged her to continue her pre-natal care as soon as she got settled in Pennsylvania.

Yesterday, the Mifflins had helped her pack the few belongings she was to carry in the car. Fortunately, the apartment was temporary and furnished and the furniture, plates, utensils and stuff like that need not be a moving problem, for they didn't belong to Sarah. The only purchase they made when they arrived a few months ago was two cheap 3' x 5' rugs for beside their bed. They hated the notion of putting their feet on the cold floor when they got out of their warm bed. They called each other 'eastern dummies', for they never thought that it could get so cold in the desert. As Mr. Mifflin put some luggage into the car,

"I got this here file box that was in my storage bin in the basement. It looks as though your teeny bin was full and Harry put this in our space. You know, we never lock it, 'cause we don't have anything of worth down there. It looks like his notes and work stuff."

"Thank you—yes, just put it in the trunk, please. I, I don't want to look at it just now."

Mr. Mifflin quickly changed the subject.

"Now, you got the auto filled up with gas and the tires and oil checked?"

"Oh, yes. My dad taught all his daughters how to take care of a car as soon as we were 16 and started to drive."

Sarah had been up since 6 AM, excited and a bit anxious, but a light breakfast and getting the last few things ready made her feel better. At about 8 AM she made her quick good-byes to the Mifflins, promised to keep in touch and was on her way. She headed out of town and toward the lake and Boulder City. She had figured that the trip was about 2300 miles and she was hopeful about making it in 4 or 5 days. Not too long later, Sarah, driving east on route 66 toward Kingman, stared out across Arizona. It was a beautifully clear day and she could see the mountains off to the left. Teary-eyed, she thought of Harry and prayed that he would return, and that the past two months had been a very bad nightmare.

### *JUNE 6, 1953: STATE COLLEGE, PENNSYLVANIA*

Sarah had taken five days coming east and she felt good that the trip was uneventful. It was approaching dusk as she pulled over at Skytop, near Bald Eagle overlook, just west of State College. She stretched as she got out of the car and walked to the railing; over to the spot where she and Harry used to look out at the Nittany Mountains which dominated the view. The last of the setting sun cast long shadows through the valley below. They used to come up here to get a burger and fries at Skytop and they never got tired of the scene. A long, deep sigh, almost unexpected, motivated her to return to the car and get to Peggy's house in town.

Fifteen minutes later she was on Atherton Street, passing College Avenue and it was like coming home. Sarah smiled, and this time her sigh was wrapped around a small smile. She made a left on Foster Street and a few blocks more and she pulled into the driveway of a small, cute house on the corner of Garner Street. Peg helped her get her three bags into the house after several screams and hugs plus a few kisses to boot. Peg took Sarah to a small second floor bedroom and they dropped all the things on the floor.

"I've got things for supper on the stove and we can talk while we eat and all night if we want, OK?"

"It sounds wonderful and I'm very happy to be here with you."

"And I'm glad you're here, and we can be great roommates again."

"Ummm . . . I think I'm going to cry, 'cause every ten

minutes, no matter what I'm doing, or saying or thinking, Harry gets into my head and I . . ."

"Listen, 'Sar', I think I can get a slight feel for what you've been through and I admit that I can't fully appreciate your situation, you know. I've never been in your shoes and all, but we're just going to get through this and I'm here to help push you through whatever and wherever."

"Oh, I know, Peggy. I, Oh, hell . . . can we eat? I'm starving and I have to catch up on getting fluids in me. The doctor said that I have to make sure I drink plenty of water."

"That's easy. Here, you sit here and I'll serve up dinner tonight and after today, we'll share everything."

During supper, Sarah related the events of the past weeks. She filled in all the empty spaces that were not covered by their brief phone conversations prior to her departure. She talked openly about the fact that one of the official theories concerned the suspicion that Harry was somehow involved in the theft of something important and highly classified. She had never doubted that this was a terrible error and Peggy, of course, mirrored her conviction that Harry was not that kind of person; never was, never is, never could be!

"Now I've got to think about getting a job, but being pregnant isn't going to make things easy. How in the world do I ask for a job, but tell them that I'm going to have a baby in January and will need three or four months off. Who would give me . . ."

"Hey, listen, I think I've got a solution to all your problems."

"What do you mean?"

"The man I work for is a great guy and very helpful. He, with the help of his wife and son, run a good deal of real estate in Centre County and they do some development."

"What kind of development?"

"The College is growing like Topsy and the need for housing is tremendous and, aside from a couple of hotels and motels, this town really needs some more places to stay for visitors parents and short time meetings and art shows and all kinds of things. Anyway, to make a very long story as short as I can, I asked him a few weeks ago about starting an adjunctive business, and told him I had this close friend that was going to live with me in the house and etc., etc., and he said go for it and he said he would even lend us some start-up cash."

"What business?"

"OK, here it is! We're going to run the business out of here, the house, and you are going to do most of the work with me backing you up. I'll still do administrative work for his company and I'll be there in the office on Brenner Pike four or five hours a day. The rest of the time, I'll be here with you."

"Hey, it sounds ideal, but would like to tell me what we'll be doing?"

"Oh, sure. We are going to publish a monthly, free, eight by ten magazine called 'On the Town'. I've got lots of contacts and will get the ad work. That's what will pay for the monthly and the profit's for us. You, my dear, will take advantage of all the four-ohs you got in all your English classes and do all the writing and editing."

"What writing?"

"We are going to list all the activities for the month, you know, movies, shows, concerts, lectures, meetings, anything. We will also list all rentals, short and long term, we will have want ads, personals, sales specials, anything that's going on in town."

"Peggy, this sounds great. It's almost like a Mickey Rooney, Judy Garland movie . . . Hey, kids, let's go to the barn and make up a show and put it on tomorrow and we'll be famous."

"Yeah, I know, it sounds weird, but tomorrow you'll see all the layouts and meet the man that will do the printing on the cuff for three months until we get up and going. My boss is buying the paper and we'll work for nothing until some bucks come in. And I've started work for us to do and we are going to publish a yearly Penn State calendar. I've got a local photographer that will give us the use of his photos and will take a commission on the sales."

"How did you manage that?"

"Every time he sees me on the street or at the diner or Corner Room, he's always leering at my behind and when I turn to look at him, he's always staring up at the sky or something. So I went to him a few weeks ago and walked in there a little more bouncy than usual and pitched the idea and, let's face it, he was hooked before I even got there. Hah! How 'bout them apples?"

"You're too much, Peggy, and I love you. You bet I'll do it with you. When the baby comes, I can work right here and be with the baby."

"We're a good team, Sarah. We were as undergrads and we are now. Come on, I'll help you unpack and I'll tell you about some other ideas that we can add on as soon as these two projects are on their feet."

*SEPTEMBER 15, 1953: STATE COLLEGE, PENNSYLVANIA*

Sarah, walking along Beaver Avenue toward home, had just left her OB-GYN office and was pleased with what she had heard. She felt good and the report corroborated the fact that she and her baby were fine. She was eating and exercising well and the work that she and Peg were doing was challenging, fun and productive. The second "On the Town" issue was due out at the end of the month for October. It had been well received and Peg had done a smash-up job in getting advertising. They had gotten the help of two grad students to do all the mock-ups for the ads. For this, they got practicum hours for their ad course and minimum wage.

Thoughts of Harry never completely left her, but being busy and laughing with Peggy was a big help and comforted her no end. They both were busy with their calendar project also. They had spent several hours and three or four meetings with Martin, the photographer, choosing the thirteen, just right, photos for the project. They had finally decided on the cover for their first edition for 1954. It would be a long shot of the Nittany Mountains, shot from the tower of Old Main. The colors were grand, for it had been a sort of strange, almost pre-stormy day. The late afternoon autumn sun had muted the colors. It was perfect and they were pleased with Martin Florin's work. The other photos were all spectacular. Some were campus scenes; one showed the corner of College and Allen Streets at about noon with plenty of people crossing the streets in front of the Corner Room. The November photo was a close-up of a football game in mid-play, taken from the sidelines. One could almost hear the clash of bodies and helmets. One of the photos, of course, had to be of the lion sculpture near Rec. Hall. The calendars would hit the streets, Sarah thought, in two of three weeks. She realized that she was even caught up in the vernacular of the trade. She had never in her life used or even thought of a phrase like 'hit the streets'!

Sarah had attended to some personal business, also. After she had settled in at Peg's and they got the projects started, Sarah had consulted a local attorney at Peg's advice. Investigators had contacted her only twice since her arrival and they wanted to remind her to call them if there was any attempt on Harry's part to contact her. Another time, they had sent someone to review all the data to date. They seemed to want all the answers from her, but they were unwilling or unable to answer any of her questions.

Her lawyer, an older, white-haired, avuncular type, was very sympathetic and listened with real interest. He advised her about putting what money she had in appropriate investments for her and the baby to come. He counseled her about a trust fund of sorts for the baby and suggested that her idea about a name change for her before the baby arrived was, indeed, a good idea. Sarah wanted to resume the use of her maiden name, Kirkendahl, for she wished to have her baby not have the possible stigma regarding the Connors name. She had been sick over this decision, for she loved Harry dearly and did not wish to hurt him, but she was sure that he would understand.

Sarah had her attorney look at the insurance policies that were Harry's. There had been two documents. One was a policy taken out by his mother when he was very young. It had been paid in full by the time he was eighteen. Presumably, it had been for college, but his mother was able to pay for his college without redeeming the policy. The other policy was from his employment with the Sandia Corporation. Sarah had the notion that she could use the cash value of the policies and put it in the trust that was suggested for the baby. She was advised, however, that since the policies were both life insurance that any access would have to be due to the death of the principal, or the principal would have to sign to release the cash value to him. Since Harry's whereabouts were unknown, nothing could be done at this time. Sarah was horrified at the thought of the attorney's next statement.

"We must wait seven years and if your husband is still missing we can then go to the courts to have him declared deceased. It's the only method of freeing any insurance funds."

It was agreed that she could come to him at any time when and if she needed him and he would write a strong letter to each of the investigation organizations requesting that any further requests to her should come to him, as her attorney.

All in all, Sarah felt fairly well, for thoughts of the baby were exciting and scary at the same time. That, and her work with Peg, was a Godsend. Some mornings she would wake and know that her dreams of Harry were not too frequent any longer, but still as strong as ever. It was as if he were still there, lying next to her, about to say, "Do I have to go to work today?".

### JANUARY 4, 1954: STATE COLLEGE, PENNSYLVANIA

Sarah and Peg had everything ready for the short ride to the hospital in Bellefonte. An old, small suitcase sat on the back seat. Peg was driving and glancing at Sarah every few moments.

"I'm not going too fast so I don't hit too many bumps real hard. Are you OK?"

"I think so. The contractions are not too severe, but even with this beach towel under me, I think I'm getting the seat wet."

"Oh, the hell with that. Don't you worry; we'll be there in a jiff."

It was typically cold, but at least there was no snow and ice. Peg made the 12 miles or so in twenty minutes and Sarah was put in a wheelchair and pushed into the emergency door as Peggy parked the car.

Less than an hour later, Adam H. Kirkendahl, six pounds, three ounces, became the newest resident of Centre County. Sarah, convinced now that all fingers, toes and everything else were there, healthy, vital and screaming for food, held Adam and smiled at Peg. In a few days the baby, the new mom and Peggy, now dubbed 'Auntie' were back at home.

\* \* \* \* \* \*

Adam grew up in a warm, loving setting. No matter how busy the women were with work, they always had plenty of time to share with Adam. He attended the Nittany Avenue public school and the local high school where he played second base on the varsity baseball team. He performed well in soccer and lacrosse, and girls would follow him with their eyes whenever he passed by. His mother noticed early on that he had his father's good nature and his frame duplicated his dad's. He parted his straight dark hair on the left and Sarah noted that he started doing that after he saw a snapshot of his father. What she never told him was that Harry 's part was on the right. He was a very good student without being dull and he, of course, wanted nothing other than Penn State. Sarah and Peg's business had flourished, so when it came time for Adam to start College, she insisted that he stay in the dorms, wisely wanting him to be as independent as possible. Adam did extremely well in biology and science and continued playing baseball throughout the four years.

All through those years, Adam was never told about the disappearance of his father. When he was old enough to ask about his father, he had been told, simply, that he had died during the Korean War. He had been shown several photos at times, and there didn't seem to be any problem or questions; at least until just after his getting his BS degree. Adam spent the week after graduation getting his things in order, for he had gotten a summer job at a neurobiology lab in Connecticut, after which he would start a Ph.D. program at the University of Pennsylvania in Philadelphia. Sarah had been nervous about telling Adam about Nevada, but she knew that she had to unburden herself and absolutely tell her son the truth. After supper one night, bolstered with a few ounces of sherry and the presence of Peggy, she told Adam the entire story. Nothing was omitted and none of it was sugar coated. It was what it was and she told him exactly that.

Adam was stunned a bit, but understood his mother's reluctance to share such information. He eased her mind by telling her that it was OK not to tell him earlier, because he could imagine that there was never a good or appropriate time to tell him. Sarah had mentioned that evening that Adam could look through his father's boxes that were in the basement. She had kept them, untouched, all those years. Adam was told, when he asked what was down there, that there was nothing of a personal nature, only files from work and that the investigators had examined the contents after the incident.

Adam slightly discomforted by the news and busy with his preparations, told his mother that he would look at the files when he returned after the summer. He left soon after, excited about the new job and being completely on his own.

### APRIL 19, 1992: STATE COLLEGE, PENNSYLVANIA

Adam stood in the familiar living room. He was in the house in which he spent all his growing years. The comfortable room was nearly the same as it was when he finished high school. Sarah was in the kitchen getting some coffee for the two of them. Adam smiled as he glanced at the pictures on the wall and a few on the mantle. Over the fireplace were three photographs from the nearby Amish area. He had always admired the quality and sensitivity of the local Bill Coleman prints. Adam had a few smaller ones at home in Philadelphia of several small Amish children. They made him smile.

Over the years since Adam was made aware of his father's history, his mother had, at times, filled in as much information as she could remember. At this point, he was comfortable with the fact that his given name had been Connors. Even though his mother was still uncomfortable with the subject, he would wonder sometimes how odd it was that in all these years, not one bit of information about his father's disappearance ever surfaced. Coffee in hand now, Sarah sat in her wing-backed chair and smiled at her handsome son.

"How was the fishing today?"

"It's always great up here, Mom. I wouldn't miss my yearly

trout visit for anything. After all, I get some good home cooking and see all my old school buddies. Spring Creek is a bit foamy from the detergent runoff, but the guys reported that the county is doing something about that. Tomorrow we'll run over toward Huntingdon to fish."

"I'm happy that you come up her often, I can't get to your place too often now. I was very glad to hear that your full professorship came through. I'm very proud of you, you know."

"Yes, I know, Mom. Thanks. I'm sure those five research papers in the Neurophysiology Journals and my last grant for six hundred thousand dollars helped. More important, what do the doctors say about your last round of chemotherapy?"

"They all agree that it's about status quo. Peggy takes good care of me and I'm able to work a few hours a day, and I like keeping busy."

"Oh, I know you like to keep busy. What was it you wanted me to clean out of the cellar?"

"I wanted to know what I should do with those old files from Nevada that belonged to your father."

"Mom, I glanced at them a bunch of years ago and there didn't seem to be anything but work notes and papers."

"Well, please do me a favor, there's only a few file boxes. Can you take them home with you and look over them more than glancing and then, if you feel there's nothing to save, you can toss them, OK?"

"Sure, Mom, I'll do that, no problem."

That night, Adam took Sarah and Peg to the Tavern for dinner. He enjoyed the place, for it conjured up lots of good times and he saw many old friends each time they went there. Sarah said that his supper order was the same each visit: a large plate of well-done nostalgia.

After his three-day visit, Adam returned to Philadelphia and, along with his bag and fishing gear, carried the few file boxes from his mother's house and put everything in his study.

The file boxes were stacked next to his desk and he quietly, on tiptoe, entered the bedroom. It was close to midnight and Fooey was sleeping, soundlessly breathing deeply, on her stomach, hugging the pillow. Adam could see the slight rhythmic movement of her back. Smiling, he backed out of the room, for he realized he wasn't sleepy enough to go to bed. He felt tired from the five-hour drive, but his head was still awake.

Adam returned to his desk and sat in his swivel chair next to the pile of file boxes. He was aware of the mustiness of the cartons and he decided to look at them quickly and get rid of them first thing in the morning. The first box contained file folders, most of which contained reprints of academic journal articles relative to electronics and engineering, all woefully out of date. Some files contained work schedules and memos of a general nature. All of these were from the U.S. Naval Base, Philadelphia, and dated around late 1952 and early 1953. The next box was half-full of notebooks from courses his father evidently took while at Penn State. There must have been twenty of them and they suffered a great deal from age. None of the spiraled books were of interest, except inside the cover of two or three Adam found his father's doodles and he was pleased that his father's favorite, based on the many repetitions, was 'HC' and 'SK' in a slightly misshapen heart. Some of the hearts had arrows through them. The rest of the carton and part of the last one contained reports of radiation levels, all coded and all dated early 1953. The last of these was dated April 6, 1953. The last of the papers were government and private organization's radiation safety information, acceptable levels, use and analysis of radiation detection devices and other related directives and reports. Adam removed a large file and read from the top sheet.

The temperature at ground level of a 15kt blast can reach 7000 degrees F. and wind velocity can be 900 miles per hour at ground zero. A mile from the blast, the wind velocity can still be 200 mph. A mid-air blast could consume the energy of Alpha and Beta rays through absorption and they would not reach the ground. Gamma and neutron rays will reach the ground and they would be extremely harmful to personnel and animals. Within 1/16th of a mile most would die immediately or soon after. Within a half-mile, most people would expire within thirty days. It is important to note that personnel entering the area within one-half mile during the initial 100 hours would be affected seriously by the radiation. The resultant . . .

Adam stopped at that point, for his eyes were beginning to droop. He bent to drop the folder back into the file box and he saw a green book lying on the bottom of the box. Apparently, the crammed-in vertical folders had hid the book, lying flat on the bottom. He picked up the book and found that it was a thin, government issued notebook. It was covered with green cloth and was about ¾ of an inch thick. On the inside cover was a hand-written note: 'Please return this logbook to Harry Connors'. The next line had been lined through with red pen, 'BOQ 15, US Naval Base', and replaced with a military style address at Desert Rock, Nevada, and an apartment address in Las Vegas, Nevada.

Adam spent the next hour reading the logbook. When he was finished, he gathered up all the files and notes on radiation data and the small green log and put them in his bottom desk drawer. The rest of the files and boxes he took out to the hallway for disposal the next day. Adam crawled quietly into bed and, as he thought about what he had read, drifted off to sleep.

*APRIL 20, 1992: PHILADELPHIA, PENNSYLVANIA*

It was a workday, early morning and still dark in the bedroom that Adam shared with his long-time love, Fooey Ginsberg.

The nickname was an old family thing started by her little brother many years ago when he couldn't pronounce Florence. Fooey was pleased about this, for she felt that her given name belonged to someone several decades older and with hair tied in a bun at the back of her head. A Ph.D. in biochemistry, she invariably signed her articles and everything else with just her initial, 'F'.

Adam had just yielded to his usual early morning testosterone rush, always much to the joy of Fooey. He lay sprawled over her, breathing calmly and kissing her neck. Fooey sighed and whispered,

"I think you fell out!"

"Au contraire, madam, I think you fell off!"

"My, my, what a bunch of pretentious crap."

"OK—so now I have a hardoff; what are you going to do about it? You going to sue me or something, huh?"

She laughed her chuckly laugh and pushed him to the side, jumped out of bed and ran to the bathroom.

Adam loved Fooey like no one else, ever. They had been together for over five years and he had asked her to marry more times than he could remember. She was quite happy to be where they were and she had promised, with her kisses, assuring him that as soon as she felt a great a need for some children in their life, they would do the deed. She was the only woman that he ever knew that laughed and smiled when she awakened. Never allowing her degrees and academic position to get in the way, Fooey was forever kibitzing and very often made fun of herself. She loved Adam's easy aura and personality and always funned him about how weird he was. At the first Passover dinner that he had been invited to by her parents, he broke up her father by singing a song he wrote for the occasion. With a fairly clear voice, he sang his immortal, 'I've got those Matzohdickah blues, which rhymes with Jews, and I haven't crapped in a week'

This, of course, endeared him to her father and produced

THE SEARCH FOR HARRY C

funny looks from her mother and sisters. Fooey's dad was not beyond the bizarre, either, for he immediately retold his favorite local story about wanting to open a dairy product store in the small town where they lived about an hour north of Philadelphia. He wanted to call the store 'The Cheeses of Nazareth'.

Over their morning coffee, Adam related what he had learned from the logbook he had found to Fooey, for he needed her as a sounding board. He trusted her judgment. Actually, he told himself almost daily, that he was very lucky, indeed, to have found her. The one overriding thing she taught him, more important than anything, was that the essence of love was simple, honest and easy. He told her also of the sadness and sorrow that he felt and for his mother, living with these secrets for so long, and about her tears when she pleaded with Adam to believe that his father was not a traitor. Her admonishing him not to think ill of him, and to trust her judgment about what a good person he had been, echoed resonantly in his mind. Fooey had listened intently, while all the time holding his hand.

"I never knew him and I have this great urge to do something, but I don't know what."

"I would support anything you wanted to do ..."

"To find out something about him, or what happened in Nevada somehow might help—hell, I just don't know!"

"Well, think about it and we'll talk as much and as often as we have to, and if you want to find out more, that's what we'll do. I can help too, you know?"

Adam kissed her cheek and smiled.

"How very lucky I am, I am!"

*MAY 30, 1992: PHILADELPHIA, PENNSYLVANIA*

At Hahnemann, like all medical academic institutions, May was always very hectic and probably the worst of all months.

Adam was as busy as everyone else what with end of the academic year exams, papers, final dissertation reviews, budget projections for next year, last-quarter research reports and an inordinate number of stupefying meetings. Winding down for the usually slower summer activities was the prize for all the work this month. In addition, Adam and Fooey had spent several hours during the month reading Adam's father's log. Some of it was straightforward and easily understood, other notations were difficult to decipher. Harry had used, at times, some of his own shorthand, or it seemed that way. They were both researchers, so it was instinctive for them to examine the log in a very rational way. They agreed on a simple plan for the examination and analysis of their findings. Fooey was the first to question the fact that the log was, obviously, at the bottom of that file box all these years and if it was there before Adam's Mom left Nevada, how come the investigators didn't find it and confiscate it?

"I'll call my Mom and ask her."

"No, wait for a while and let's see if we develop more questions to ask her, otherwise we'll be calling every hour and upset her more than need be, OK?"

"Wise advice, as usual. What else do we have?"

That evening, they called State College after dinner. Sarah had been told early in the month about the log.

"I've been thinking about the little book you found and I sort of remember that Harry had a book like that and he would carry it in his pocket to work sometimes."

"Mom, we have a few questions."

"All right."

"The investigators, you know, like the FBI guys and the military people, did they ever ask you about the log?"

"Not that I remember."

"Where were the file boxes kept, in the apartment?"

"No, both the boxes were kept in our little storage space in the basement."

"And did the people that came and looked around the apartment look at those boxes?"

"Yes, I told them they were there and we went down there and they looked through the boxes and other things that were there."

"What other things?"

"Well, we had some old empty suitcases and we kept some cleaning things for the house and your father had a bucket and car wax and rags he used to wash and shine the car, nothing very important."

"Wait a minute, you said both file boxes and I had three boxes. Are you sure you only had two?"

"Oh! Mr. Mifflin had a box of Harry's in his space."

"Miffler, who's that?"

"No, Mifflin, with an 'n' on the end . . . they were our neighbors in the building, very nice and very thoughtful. They took me to their doctor when I was ill and I found out I was carrying you."

"OK, right, but what did you mean that he had a box."

"I recall clearly that he helped me pack up the car and he had a box in his little space in the basement. He said something about that your father asked if he could keep it in his space, because we had no more room and Mr. Mifflin said it was OK."

"Did you know about the box being there when you took the investigators down there?"

"No, I didn't. I never knew until the day I left and if it weren't for the old man telling me, I would have never known."

"Wow, then the investigators only looked in your basement space and they never knew that the third box was there. Do you think that's plausible?"

"I would imagine that it's very possible. They spent about an hour down there and they took several files and gave me a receipt, but I don't think they ever returned anything to me."

"Fooey's on the extension in the bedroom and . . ."

"Hello, Fooey dear, how are you?"

"I'm fine Sarah, are you being diligent about your medication and diet?"

"Yep. My doctor's very pleased with the vitamin regimen you suggested and I do feel much more energized during the day. You know, I even sleep better. I think that with more energy during the day, I'm getting more active and with more activity I sleep better. Does that make sense?"

"It sure does, and I'm glad to hear that. Listen, before I forget, Adam and I came across the initials 'DDT' in the log, does that mean anything to you?"

"Mmm, not off hand, I don't . . . wait a minute, I remember some of the boys in the fraternity may have called Dick Tishman 'DDT'.

"I can understand the 'DT', but maybe his middle name began with a 'D'."

"I wouldn't have known that, I think."

"Did Harry ever speak to you about the work here at the Naval Base or the stuff he was doing in Nevada?"

"Hardly at all. He did say several times that the work they were doing was classified and secret, so he rarely spoke about it. I only remember that once or twice he would come home when we were in Las Vegas and he would seem upset."

"Do you know about what?"

"I recall that he was mumbling about the radiation intensities and the build-up of doses, one time. It never made sense to me and he was never mad for long. He was really a very easygoing and sometimes, even, a passive kind of man."

"How do you mean?"

"Well, like he wouldn't go out of his way to be confrontational, like some people. He would speak up when he had to, but never with malice or he wasn't a hateful kind of person either."

"Mom, I'd like you to do me a favor when you get off the phone."

"Of course, what?"

"Spend a few days and think of any names from the fraternity that you remember and write them down. Then, please send them to me. OK?"

"Yes, of course. What do you plan to do with the names?"

"I'm going to try to contact some of them and I guess I want to start developing some background information. I really want to follow through with this and I, we, Fooey and I, want to see if we can find out what happened out in Nevada. I want to do this, but not at your expense, Mom. I don't want this to make you feel bad or get in a funk over this."

"Don't you worry about me, Adam. If you two want to do this, then go to it. I told you before that I feel good about your wanting to find out more about your father."

"OK, as long as you assure me that you will not have any negative consequences from this."

"Adam, listen. I'm sure that some of the information you find will take me back into the middle of that mess and I'm sure it will bring up some bad memories, but there were plenty of good memories that will balance out those bad ones. Just promise me that you will keep me posted about what you find and try not to spare my feelings, OK?"

"You're on, Mom, and you're swell and pretty good lookin' for an old broad."

"Hey, watch what you say, young man."

"OK, OK, will do. We'll be off now and we'll speak to you soon."

"Bye, Sarah. We'll come up and visit real soon."

"You do that and I'll do up some of my best chicken and dumplings for you both. Peggy sends love. Bye-bye."

123

*JUNE 12, 1992: PHILADELPHIA, PENNSYLVANIA*

The two of them sat facing each other at the small table for two directly in front of the fireplace in the back of Sassafras on Second Street. Bobby had just placed a glass of white wine and a Rolling Rock beer on their table. Fooey put her hand over Adam's.

"What?"

"Huh?"

"You look pensive, what are you thinking about?"

"Oh, nothing important. I was wondering what I should do about the few names my Mom sent. You know, the guys she remembers from the fraternity."

"You're going to find them and see some of them, right?"

"Sure, and she really saved us some trouble. She called the frat up there and got their president on the phone and he said he would contact the fraternity's national office to see if they had addresses on some of those that she remembered. He gave her three names and current addresses in his mailing list."

"So what do you have now?"

"Mom had mentioned Dick Tishman several times before, so I know where he is, and she sent me the three others."

"Are they close by?"

"Yes. A few of them are here in the city, one in Cherry Hill and Tishman's info I dug out of the library computer at work."

"Is this the guy that has a Ph.D. and was a close friend of your Dad's?"

"Yes, wait, I have one of the pages from the printout. Here it is, listen."

United States Academy of Sciences Elects New Senior Fellows.

The Academy elected four Fellows at a meeting of its council on Friday, April 17, 1985. The elected scholars include Dr. Anthony Hispanya, Stanford University, Dept. of . . .

"Where's Tishman's name?"

"Here it is."

Richard M. Tishman, Princeton University, Department of Physics . . .

"His initials are 'RMT', so we're not sure if the 'DDT' refers to him or not, even though your Mom seems to remember that it may. You could get up to see him easily, were you able to find him?"

"That was easy. I called the department at Princeton and I was told that he was an emeritus professor now and he was still in the community. She wouldn't give me his address, but I found it in the phone book."

"Hey, good work. You're a real Perry Mason. When are you going up there? It's only about thirty or forty minutes, I think. Should I come too?"

"I'll call him and find out when I can get up there at his convenience and then we can decide about the two of us going. Is that OK with you?"

"Absolutely. Hey, here comes dinner."

While eating, Adam told Fooey about the Tishman biography he had found in "Who's Who in Science."

"It's amazing how little effort it takes to get information. This bio gave me everything except his mother's maiden name and his blood type."

"So what's important, you know, just the facts, ma'am stuff."

"Nothing out of the ordinary. He worked for Sandia, but we know that, and then he went to France for his Ph.D.; he spent about five years there. No mention of a wife or family and his early work was in Atomic Physics, radiation and a mix of electronics and acoustics."

"What kind of mix is that? That's something you don't hear about."

"Some mention about acoustic-driven trigger mechanisms."

"Triggers for what?"

"The bio didn't go into any detail, so I made a quick request for articles, all the academic articles from any journals authored by Tishman and any he co-authored."

"Hell, you could get a truckload."

"Yeah, well, I've got to start somewhere and you'll give me a hand sorting things out. The bio indicated that his name is on about forty-five articles, chapters in sixteen texts and he authored four textbooks. The last one is still used in Princeton's Graduate School."

"You'll give me some and I'll help you wade through them. We just have to agree at the outset about what we're looking for and what's pertinent. Can we do that?"

"We'll certainly try. I'll start to make some calls tomorrow and set up some meetings with the local guys that were in the fraternity."

Fooey mumbled an assent as she chewed on the last of her stir fry and got the last few drops of the wine by tilting the glass up like she was balancing it on her lips. Bobby saw this and asked if they wanted more to drink and they settled on two coffees and no dessert.

They walked the few blocks back to their apartment hand in hand, quiet, happy and full.

### JUNE 18, 1992: CHERRY HILL, NEW JERSEY

Adam sat in the office of Marty Harris, an Optometrist and old fraternity brother of Harry Connors. Marty had agreed to see Adam at the end of the workday.

"Holy mackerel, it must be almost thirty-six or seven years since I saw your Dad—and I was sorry to hear that he's gone."

"Gone is probably the appropriate word here, Dr. Harris."

"Please, please—call me Marty."

"Sure, Marty, thanks. You see, my father is legally deceased and aside from what my Mom has in the way of information about him, I have damned little else. I wanted to get some more info about him from some people that knew him. I know it's a long shot, but my fiancee and I want to try and find out what happened to him. You said on the phone that you knew him pretty well at Penn State."

"I certainly did. We hooked up during registration week and we lived on the same floor of the temporary dorms. He even took me home to his Mom's place for dinner a couple of times. I remember his mother, a nice lady. Did you know her?"

"No, never."

"Anyway, it was funny. I asked her once how come she wanted Harry to be in the dorms instead of at home and his Mom, I guess, your Grandmother, said that he'd be more independent and also get to meet good-looking guys like me."

"Interesting, that, 'cause that's exactly why my Mom wanted me in the dorms. I mean, not to meet other people, but to grow up a bit more."

"Your Dad and I were rushed by the same frats and we both decided on the same one, along with some other fellows in the dorms."

"Can you remember some names for me?"

"Let's see—some of the boys that started together—let's see. Oh, sure, Tinkleman, and Soffert, the short guy that played baseball, Irving and Tishman. There was a guy who put a microphone in the lady's room during a party—Porter, yeah, Joe Porter. I'm picturing some of them, but the names are not coming. Wait a second, Dan Silvers—he arranged a big Saturday night barn dance during Spring Week. What a fun thing that was. He rented a local farmer's barn and we all went out there and cleaned it up for the party. We put in fresh hay up on the lofts and Dan hires a band and they dressed up in farm kinda clothes and somebody made a big painted sign out front of the barn that said, 'The Bar-Mitzvah Ranch.' I remember that Dan lost his glasses rolling around the loft with his date and they never did find them. Dan even had a hay wagon carry us all in shifts to the barn. Boy, was that fun! Well, that's been lots of years ago and I guess that kind of information is not helping you, is it."

"No, no, not at all. Anything from those days can be helpful. Just getting little bits of data gives me a better handle on my father. Can you tell me about him?"

"Of course. Harry was a nice-looking guy and he was very well liked because he was genuinely honest, straight forward and an all-around nice person. He was always helping other guys, and even got some of us to go over to the hospital in Bellefonte to paint the walls of six wards for our pledge project. I'm not telling you bull because you're sitting here and I want to please you. He was a good friend and a great young man."

"That's nice to hear, I appreciate it. Anything else?"

"I remember that he dated fairly often and we both worked."

"Where did you work?"

"We waited tables at DTD and . . ."

"Wait, did you say DDT?"

"No, I said 'DTD', that's a frat name, Delta Tau Delta. We waited tables and got all our meals free. We did that for two years or so and then I stopped working and then your Dad got a job as a waiter at the Dutch Pantry. That's about the time he and your Mom met and started dating. Boy, did he ever smile a lot and your Mom too. They were a Hollywood pair, just seemed to be meant for each other. What a sweety she was. On the phone you told me she still lived in State College, huh?"

"That's right, she does."

"Please tell her that I said hello and ask if she remembers me. She was one pretty and special young lady, I'll tell ya."

---

"Thank you, I'll be sure to tell her. By the way, Marty, do the initials 'DDT' mean anything to you?"

"You mean besides the bug spray they use for crops?"

"Yes."

"Not off hand, no."

"I called Dr. Tishman the other day and I'm scheduled to see him in Princeton soon."

"Oh, is that where he is now?"

"Yes, he's retired from the University and he lives up there. I don't think he's married or anything like that."

"It's no wonder!"

"What do you mean, didn't you like him?"

"Sort of yes and sort of no."

"Go on, please. I assure you I'll keep it confidential."

"Well, he always had a nice guy front, but a lot of us knew that there was a nefarious side to him: you know, if there was a corner to cut, he cut it; if there was a scam around something, he did it; and I even recall that a few of us thought that he wasn't very trustworthy, particularly in card games."

"What else?"

"He was also not very nice to the girls, like he treated them like things or dolls and wasn't nice and honest with them, like calling off a date at the last minute because he found someone else he thought was better in some way. People became, as they got to know him, somewhat circumspect about him. He wasn't the kind of guy that would fight or hit anybody or steal, you know. He was outwardly pleasant and often fun to be with. Some of the guys were happy that he took a year away, I think in our junior year, to spend in France, I think. When he came back I remember that somebody said that he came back the same, but now he does it in French."

"Did he room with my father any time?"

"Mmm, yeah, for a little bit, I think. I'm not really sure, now that I think about it."

---

129

"Do you keep in touch with anyone from those days?"

"I speak only to Heshy, my old roommate, about once a month. He's in California, in Newport Beach, a VP in an ad-marketing firm. We see each other at least once a year. I go there, he comes here, we even met each other once in New Orleans, you know, with our wives."

The two continued to chat for another ten minutes and Marty took Adam's number. Adam said his thanks and headed back toward the Benjamin Franklin Bridge and home.

He was a bit frustrated about the meeting, for he wanted to find out all sorts of important things in this short first interview. He realized that this was an unrealistic expectation born of his excitement and great motivation to get some answers. As he approached the tollbooths, he turned his mind to some of the work he had to complete that was piled-up on his desk at the Medical School.

## *JUNE 27, 1992: BALA CYNWYD, PENNSYLVANIA*

Adam held the steering wheel of his car tightly as he negotiated the extreme curve coming off the expressway and onto City Line Avenue. He left the city as he made his first right turn and picked up speed. His meeting this afternoon was with another of his father's fraternity brothers, Phil Noonan, who insisted that he would be pleased to see Adam as long as they could meet at the Deli on Montgomery Avenue.

The parking lot behind the Deli was almost full when Adam arrived, but he squeezed into a spot between two large black cars. Waiting inside were several people and one of them a tall, thin, well-dressed man of the appropriate age smiled as Adam entered. Hellos were exchanged and the two men were led to a booth where the smell of garlic and the pickle brine almost made Adam sneeze. As soon as they were seated, their orders were taken and,

"So, you're Harry's son."

"Yes, sir, that's me."

"On the phone you mentioned that you never knew your father, right?"

"True, he disappeared before I was born."

"The story you told me certainly intrigued me. You mean that your mother never heard anything about the results of the investigation?"

"No, sir, not a word after the first year or so. Then, nothing. As far as we know, the case was never closed or there was nothing more to report."

"Yikes, that's really eerie. How can I help?"

"I've seen one of your old school chums and I will see another soon, and I merely wish to get some background on my father. I never had a feeling for what he was like and who his friends were."

"Who did you see so far?"

"Marty Harris and I met last week in Cherry Hill."

"He was a good old boy and I remember him well. My memory is clear because we used to have weekly poker games in his room. I realize now that I was a terrible poker player. We only played for nickels but I usually lost five or six bucks each time."

"I'm scheduled to see Dr. Tishman soon also."

"Ah, yes, dear Dr. Tishman, I remember him well also. I read some time ago that he had a very prestigious position at Princeton and he's had several noteworthy awards bestowed. Quite a guy!"

"How so?"

"Not important now, I guess."

"I assure you, sir, that whatever you say will be between us."

"Tishman was entertaining and he was always pleasant and good company, but he was an opportunist, a disingenuous fellow and filled with knavery. I love words, by the way.

I always wanted to be a writer. I was a business major at State, but I minored in Theater and English."

"That's nice, Mr. Noonan, but is there anything else you can recall?"

"Only that I thought he cheated at cards, but maybe he was just good. I sure wasn't. Actually, it's not fair of me to accuse him, after all, he probably took our money honestly because he was a good card player."

"Mr. Noonan, do the initials 'DDT' mean anything to you, from back then at Penn State, I mean?"

"Sure it does, and some coincidence."

"What coincidence?"

"A few of the guys dubbed Tishman with the 'DDT' thing."

"Dr. Tishman? His initials are 'RMT', I believe."

"Nah, it had nothing to do with his name, but rather his great science background. He was one big braggadocio."

"You mean he bragged and honked his own horn often."

"Often and loudly, right! The 'DDT' came about at one of the dinners at the frat. For some reason there were an inordinate amount of flies and Tishman went around the room clapping his hands and killing nearly all the flies."

"I don't understand, how did he do that?"

He lectured all of us watching him that when a fly takes off, because of its structure, it takes off in a backward direction, then goes forward. If you clap your hand behind the fly as he takes off, you squoosh him. He must have done that to twenty or thirty of them. After that several of the fellows mocked him by calling him 'DDT'. I never wanted to shake his hand after that, but he was right, I've tried it many times."

Noonan and Adam, during the remainder of their lunch, talked about Harry. Adam was, essentially, told the same thing as Marty Harris had described. His father was a prince of a guy, always pleasant, helpful, a good friend, reliable and Adam was told that the Boy Scout oath was probably mostly made with Harry in mind. Adam was asked about his Mom and his work at Hahnemann. He was also offered any help he needed from Noonan.

"Listen, Adam, I own one of the largest commercial publishing houses in this area and if you need some help with resources, searches, data collecting or whatever, you come to me. Keep my number, do ya hear?"

Noonan insisted he pay for lunch and Adam assured him that he would ask for assistance if need be. A promise to keep him informed was also made.

As he made his way back to the Schuylkill Expressway, Adam was pleased that, at least, one small puzzle was solved. He knew who 'DDT' is. What it meant was another story, but he and Fooey would discuss things and figure out how to proceed. Adam slowed as he left the on ramp and then sped up to join the parade of cars all intent, it seemed, to get him. As he relaxed from the minor ordeal, he wondered what the hell 'Schuylkill' meant.

### JULY 4, 1992: PHILADELPHIA, PENNSYLVANIA

Fooey was in the kitchen boiling a large pot of potatoes and water and listening to the ten AM news on the radio. She and Adam had finished a late breakfast and they were preparing for their usual Fourth of July mid-city type barbecue. Every year they invited eight or nine couples to their Old City loft apartment for fried chicken, corn on the cob, potato salad, cole slaw, sodas, beer and whatever anyone else brought to the party. During the first few years of what became a yearly thing, Fooey had labored long and hard, particularly with the fried chicken. Adam, several years back, suggested that they try Kentucky Fried Chicken, and that worked out just fine. So, every year since, while Fooey set about preparing the other stuff and putting out all the disposable paper plates and cups, Adam would drive to Oregon Avenue and load up with

133

the take-out chicken and pick up bags of ice for the drinks. Their friends were mostly people from work and several neighborhood pals and they all gathered on the roof late in the evening to watch the fireworks over the Delaware River.

"Adam, I'm almost finished examining Harry's log and there are several things we should talk about."

"Sure. I came up with some strange things too, you know, it seems funny that he used the log for work notes and comments; sort of like a personal diary and memos to himself and he noted a lot of stuff about his digging jaunts in Nevada too."

"What was that fellow's name, the one your Mom mentioned that Harry and Tishman went out on digs with?"

"Mickey Haws. His name is in the log several times, even the driving directions to his trailer the first time they found him. What things did you question that you found?"

"OK. First: Harry notes more than a couple of times that he's concerned about the radiation levels. After you spend some time with the log you can get the gist of his simple shorthand, well, sometimes, at least. Anyway, he indicates that Radiation Tags weren't worn by some or, in one instance, none of the troops involved in the tests had them."

"Are those the 'rad-tags' he mentions, like the dental x-ray, white things?"

"Yes, I'm sure they were in use then. They were the simplest and cheapest way to detect radiation. The tags had to be examined very often and in some cases, every day. Otherwise, you couldn't tell when and where the exposure took place."

"Harry seemed to be very worried that overexposure was taking place and he specifically wrote that nobody responded to his fears, Tishman, written 'DDT', among them."

"Right, he wrote that 'DDT' rejected the notion out of hand and he then jotted down about a half page of radiation data, conversion figures and a very brief discussion of the immediate and long-range effects. He compared his data with the official data being reported to the government and the latter figures were not as serious-sounding as Harry's."

"I picked up on that, too, and I compared some of Harry's notes and figures with some of Tishman's early articles in the journals we started to get from the library and guess what?"

"OK, what?"

"There are several sentences and data configurations that are almost exact duplicates of the official reports that Harry mentions in the log relative to his findings of inconsistencies."

"Last week I researched some stuff and compared Harry's data with present data and, get this, the one-day exposure by the troops and others taking part in the Nevada shots were considered safe then, but today, that same exposure level is acceptable for an entire year for a nuclear employee."

"God! A whole year?"

"Yep, a whole year. I even found some veteran's groups that are formally trying to get benefits because of related cancers and other illnesses."

"I'm calling Tishman this week, after the weekend, and going up there to see him. I've been trying lately, but he doesn't seem to have an answering machine."

"What about Mickey Haws, will you see him too?"

"Mom mentioned him several times. She said that she met him once or twice and he and Harry got pretty tight and Harry went out digging with him more than Tishman did. Of course, they went out together often, too. I don't know what he can offer, but we won't know unless I try. Did you notice that Harry drew some petroglyphs in his log and noted the approximate places they were found, and the date he saw them?"

"Sure I did. Those dates give the log some time structure. We can assume that his notes, many undated, were at least written in the order that we see them. In mixing up what he was writing about, be it work stuff, his diary and his digging log, we have some idea of chronology. Here, look at the log and the Indian signs. Look, here's one that looks like three spearheads pointing upward, and this one appears to be steps, five or six of them rising from left to right . . ."

"That one I remember from one of my undergrad courses. It means, I think, that there's a way out going up, you know, like start climbing up here and you can leave the canyon or something. They had a water sign, too, but I don't remember what that was."

"Look at this small spiral and what looks like a spirochete approaching it. What do you think?"

"Lord knows. I think we can be safe in our assumption that the Indian signs have little to do with our search, huh?"

"Just to be sure, I photocopied them and faxed them to North Carolina to the Indian Museum in Frisco and Carl there will tell us if they make any sense or they're just random sightings."

"Sounds good, Foo, that's smart. Hey, that pot is boiling over."

"Thanks, and stick around, you can give me a hand and peel those things when they cool down."

### JULY 22, 1992: PRINCETON, NEW JERSEY

Adam and Fooey had driven up Route 95 to Jersey and then onto 206 in well under an hour. Adam slowed down at the sign warning drivers to do so as they entered the pretty little town.

"There's a great deal of history here, you know?"

"How do you mean, Adam?"

"Well, everyone that was anyone's been here to teach or to be a visiting lecturer, like Albert Einstein on down."

"Well, many of the modern locals would have it, like, from Einstein on up!"

"No doubt, you're right. We're on the main drag and what

next? He gave me rather sketchy instructions. He didn't seem overly excited about our visit, I had to pull an acceptance out of him."

"The University's on the right and go on straight until, well, keep on and I'll tell you where to turn left."

A few minutes later, Adam pulled over in front of a small, well-kept cottage on a tree-lined narrow street. Fooey observed that if a place tried to look like a perfect little University of the Ivy League type, they would make a copy of this street."

A light tap on the door beckoned their arrival and as the door swung open they saw a balding, slightly stooped man that looked older than his sixty years.

"Dr. Tishman, I'm Adam Kirkendahl and this is my fiancé, Florence Goldberg. We spoke on the phone the other day."

"Yes, of course, please come in. I was just watering my plants."

"Here, have a seat in the sunroom and I'll join you in a moment."

Tishman continued down the short hall and went into the back room.

"Hey, smartass, what's with the 'Florence'? You know I hate that."

"Hey, I wanted to be a bit formal, we don't know this guy. All I wanted to do was . . ."

"Ah, here we are. I'm sorry I couldn't get you up here sooner, but I've been out of the country for a few weeks. So, you're Harry's son. And how is Sarah?"

"She's doing OK, sir, and she is still living in State College, as I mentioned on the phone. I also mentioned that we're looking for information about my father."

"So you said when we spoke, but I'm not sure what information you had in mind and I can't see how I can be of help after all these years."

"Sir, I never knew my father, as you are well aware, and

137

the only information that I have is, basically, from my mother. We know that he disappeared and my mother thinks that the government felt that he had stolen some secret or something important. She was ordered not to speak to anyone about the investigation that went on and she remembered that they told her they were treating their investigation as a missing person case."

"That's what I recall also. There wasn't much to it. Except, of course, for the fact that Harry never surfaced again."

"My mother's lawyer got the government to agree in their attempt to get papers for legal death status so she could settle some of his affairs."

"Mmm, I see. I was a close friend of Harry's from the start at Penn State. We were fraternity brothers and we spent a lot of time together. We double dated a lot had fun and went to Philadelphia to the Navy yard together to work after we started together at Sandia in New Mexico. I'm sure your mother told you that I was the best man at their wedding."

"Yes, sir, she did. She has shown me several pictures. She doesn't take them out too often."

"No, I suppose not. Young lady, I know your name. I reviewed several Biophysics articles last year and I was most impressed with your work. Hahnemann should be proud to have you."

"Thank you, Dr. Tishman. I would hope the Chair of my department feels the same when my salary review comes up in the fall."

The next few minutes were taken up with some questions about Harry. Tishman was told of Adam's visits to a couple of frat brothers in the area and Tishman certainly gave Harry the same kind of kudos that Phil Noonan and Marty Harris had. Tishman also went on and on about he felt so poorly about his not keeping in touch with Sarah and getting to know Adam. He also stated that he felt that Harry would have been the last person that anyone would expect to do anything underhanded.

"It sounds as though you think he was, indeed, guilty of something, even though you think that he doesn't fit the bill as a heavy."

"I don't know. I really can't believe or, er, don't believe it."

"What was taken or stolen or whatever?"

"Most of the material has been declassified, so I can tell you without any further detail that the most modern U.S. nuclear trigger mechanism at that time was stolen."

"You mean the actual device was missing?"

"No, no, a rough draft and schematic, or rather a copy was missing at the same time as Harry's disappearance."

"Sir, we have Harry's personal logbook and we've got some questions."

"Go ahead."

"He wrote of two strange incidents that concerned having notes taped to his desk. Both notes indicated that 'DDT' called and wanted Harry to review some data that you had and Harry could find on your desk. Both times he had been looking on your desk and you were confrontational about his rummaging on or in your desk. One note indicated that the idea of getting a note was thought to be a fabrication. You were called, at times, at the frat, 'DDT', correct?"

"Yes, I was, at times. At least for a little while, yes. I don't know what to make of these notes of Harry's. I really don't remember."

"Other notes refer to Harry's feeling that there were irregularities regarding radiation levels. He notes a few times that he discussed this with you and a naval officer named Spearson. He further indicated that he had sent formal reports about what he thought were serious radiation level errors. I believe in other sections Spearson is referred to as Puffy."

"Yes, I do remember that situation. It seemed that when

ALTS

it came to radiation, Harry was something of a Cassandra and his thinking was specious but, in truth, revealed itself to be spurious and groundless, I would say."

"But, sir, we've reviewed most of your journal articles and texts over the past weeks, and in one article that appeared quite early in your career, you wrote at length about gamma and neutron rays, the so-called very harmful rays. And in so doing, you seem to have lifted several sentences and illustrations directly from the notes and reports of Harry's. Please excuse me, sir, I'm not making accusations, I'm just damn curious."

"Well, I'm sure that many coincidences occur. After all, your father and I worked closely together and we collaborated in what eventually became articles that I authored. I may have been a bit hasty in removing Harry's name from the work and perhaps it was bad judgment on my part. He was missing, you see."

"Certainly, I see, but my question is not one that is concerned about some data or being used. In 1953 you thought that Harry's ideas about radiation irregularities and the non-use of rad-tags, etcetera, had no genuine worth. You said that it was really false and not plausible. In your article, however, Harry's data are used to support your discussion. That's the crux of our confusion."

"I can see how, indeed, that one could be confused. But please note, a few years had passed and at the time of publication, several radiation standards had been struck down and new ones put in place. Also, different and radical theories of gamma and neutron rays, that is the half-lives and the ratios of harmful effects, had changed drastically also."

"Are you saying that some or all of what Harry discerned may have been valid?"

"Yes, in part, yes. Certainly some may have been correct."

Adam and Fooey spent another ten or fifteen minutes

groping for something, but to no avail. Tishman remembered Commander Spearson, several of the senior technicians, one or two navy enlisted men and a few people from Sandia, but hadn't seen any of them since his departure many years ago to earn his doctorate degree in France. They took their leave and drove slowly through the town, heading back toward Route 95.

"Adam, the old duck, in the hour we were there, never offered us a drink of water or anything. I don't think he was used to company at all. He seemed like a loner."

"You're right and he seemed like a disenchanted man, without energy, like he was deflated."

"Sure as hell not the kind of man that you could have fun with, that's for sure."

"Maybe we read him wrong, you know. He's sixty-ish and maybe he's ill or something. But, after all, with all his honors, his achievements and all, I would expect that he would feel rewarded and good about himself. Oh, hell, who knows?"

"Do me a favor, my man, please stop for something cold before we hit 95. I need to drink something and also pee!"

### AUGUST 16, 1992: NEVADA ROUTE 25, NORTH

Adam had left Las Vegas behind him about 100 miles ago and was driving over several 5000-foot peaks on his way to Route 6 and the town of Blue Jay. He was fortunate that Harry's log helped in finding Mickey Haws. Adam and Fooey had, at first, tried to find his phone number through the information service using several towns in the vicinity with no luck. They worried that the man may have died and they even tried the Social Security and the Veterans offices, but they were not permitted to get that kind of information because of privacy laws. The same went for the state of Nevada. The Bureau of Vital Statistics in Carson City couldn't give out any information either. Nothing could be divulged about

141

a driver's license or real estate tax info. It was Fooey that recalled the radio call sign that Harry and Tishman used to contact Haws in the fifties. It was in Harry's notebook. They went to a friend, a ham radio nut, and he used the call sign for several days, at different times of the day and, bingo! The friend found Mickey Haws in Blue Jay. Arrangements were made for Adam to visit and with what was supposed to be part of their summer vacation money, a round-trip air ticket and a rental car was arranged.

A sign announcing 'Route 6 The Grand Army of the Republic Highway' prompted Adam to hang a right for what his map indicated was the last dozen miles to Blue Jay.

Mickey had given Adam good instructions to the house that Mickey had been raised in and the instructions were hardly necessary, for the town was so small that it would have been impossible to get lost. Mickey was found in the shade of the back porch with a beer, staring out at the rough desert expanse.

"Hi there, Mickey, I'm glad to see you. I'm Adam Kirkendahl."

"I guess you would be, man. I'm glad to see you too. Sit down a bit. Want a cold beer? There's a few in the fridge in there."

"Thanks, I will."

"So, you're Harry's son! Well, hell, you got some of his looks, that's for sure."

"I do, huh? Is that good?"

"Sure is. Your Dad was a good guy and he had a nice nature, quiet like, but when he said stuff you could listen and know it counted for something. We was good friends and we had lots of good times digging and hiking. Dick was with us too, but your Dad was the good guy."

"What do you mean, Mickey?"

"Harry, you see, was the kind of friend that helped a person without telling him so."

"Like how do you mean?"

"He always bought more things than we needed for the trip, like food and beer and such, so he could leave it with me when they went back to the base. And they always gave me what we dug, so I could sell some things. That was your Dad's idea, not Tishman."

"What was Tishman like?"

"OK, I guess, but he always had an edge on him I didn't care for. I thought the story that Harry ran off with something was a lot of bushwa! Never believed that for one second, never!"

"Why did you think that?"

"A man can get a fix on a person and ya just can size some people up real good and Harry was not the kind of man to do a thing like they said. And he was always considerate. Like if we got late, he would worry about your Mom and call her as soon as we got to someplace with a phone. Your Mom was a sweetheart. She fed us a few times when they took me to town now and again. I even stayed over at your folks' place a couple of times."

"She's still like that and she remembers you well."

"You be sure to say hi there for me, sure?"

"Yes, sir, I will."

"Grab us two more beers and I'll show you some things."

"Right, and I'll use your facilities also, if you don't mind."

"You do that, and I'll go to the shed and get a box with some things I found for you."

Back on the porch, Mickey spoke about his life in the desert and his trailer overlooking the river. He told Adam that he moved into the family home that his father had built as a young man. It had been empty for a few years and he was getting more bound up with arthritis and the start of what the VA doctors thought was emphysema. He couldn't go digging in the hills anymore, so he retired from his retirement.

"I remember them investigators coming out to see me three or four times and pretty much asking me them same questions. They even asked if they could look around my trailer and the big lean-to I had out back there."

"What for?"

"Damn if I know. They took a good look at the jeep I used to have there and they asked if they could go inside and take a look too. They did more than that. They took fingerprint stuff from the trailer and the jeep and all, even tire track markings."

"Did they say what they were looking for?"

"Nah never did, but they spoke a bit about Harry, maybe, taking off with something. And I told them, plain like, that Harry didn't do anything like they were insinuatin'."

"Do you have any idea what could have happened back than?"

Not a clue, but one thing for sure, like the TV show I saw this week, there was something sure rotten in Denmark about the whole situation.

"How so?"

"Number one, is what I told you. Harry wasn't that kind of man. Number two, he was married to a swell woman and why would he just go off like that? Unless, maybe, somebody took him, huh? Number three, I give those FBI men some things I picked up over the next couple days after the shot, just west of the blast site, and they said they would get them back to me, but they never did."

"What kind of things?"

"I found, on the surface, no diggin' needed, a bunch of metal twisted, fused things, some charred. They took animal bones I picked up out of the same area and even a piece of a small dial-like thing that said, like, 'amp' on it. It was black with a piece of the dial like stuck on the front of it and melted-like."

"The animal bones, how did you know they were animal bones?"

"Oh, I'm sure. Been picking up stuff in the desert since I

was old enough to walk. I know the bones of all the creatures that roam around here. Look at this here in the box."

"What do we have here?"

"I had a system when I went digging. I had county plat maps that had every area sectioned off and when I found something I would mark it on the section I found it on and I dated it. I would write on the back of the map what it was that I found or dug. Then I would mark a box with the date so I could look it over later, so when I was tired or busy with something else, I could tell where and what things were."

"What are these things?"

"These are finds near the place I found the stuff that the FBI guys took and never gave back. These I found after they left. I saved these for them, but they never showed again. I had them in the lean-to behind my trailer all them years and I didn't think of them until I made the move back here, so I had all my maps and I carted all these boxes that I had left and put them in the shed back there. Here you come and ask me what can I tell you, and look at this."

"This one's a mass of metal and, whoa, this is charred like."

"Watch out for those sharp edges, one of them I got cut on."

"And this one has an animal bone, like a small shaft sticking out about three, four inches."

"Lay that down in the box, Adam. That's what I wanted to show you . . . and this other piece."

"What?"

"That's not an animal bone fragment that I know. I think that's a human fragment."

"You mean a man?"

"Or a woman, a child or who knows? Look at this piece."

"More metal, the size of my fist, twisted and . . ."

"Look at this side, into the twisted edges."

145

"Yes, there's something shiny, like an end of it is smooth and shiny."

"You bet. I've an acid tester kit for some finds and I got a small rubbing from the shiny part and it shows gold traces."

"What's your thinking on this, Mickey?"

"Well, those people were working with secret stuff and the airplanes, it wasn't no secret, even then. You could hear them screeching around the desert with those other planes following. Hell, one of those damn things buzzed me in my jeep and I almost went off the road. Your dad once mentioned something about a dummy, even. What if Harry was kidnapped for his secrets or something like that?"

"I don't know what this means, Mickey."

"OK, what if a person wanted to get rid of another person. They could put the person in a plane and then blow the thing to smithereens and no one would be the wiser, right?"

"Hell, Mickey, are you sure you don't see too much science fiction on that cable TV of yours?"

"I sure do, but it's a thought, isn't it?"

"Can I take this stuff with me? Please. I can't promise to return it, though."

"You take all you want of it."

"These few pieces will be fine, and could I make a copy of the location of the find on your map?"

"Yep. I'll get it and some paper for you. You're staying here like I asked on the phone, OK?"

"Absolutely, but I hope I can take you out for a good dinner someplace."

"You can, for sure. The bar in town serves up a very good steak."

Adam made the map copy and wrote a few notes. They both washed up at a pump at the kitchen sink. All through dinner, Mickey regaled Adam with stories of his digs with Harry and Tishman, but stories mostly about Harry. The dinner, as promised, was great and what seemed like two pounds

146

more than he usually ate. Mashed potatoes, salad, two beers and apple pie and coffee. Hell, he was stuffed, but he didn't care.

That night, he fell asleep thinking about Mickey's finds and in a few moments he was snoring. Too much beer always did that. The next morning he made his goodbye and headed back to the city for the flight back home, but not before he stashed two six-packs of beer in Mickey's refrigerator.

### *AUGUST 21, 1992: PHILADELPHIA, PENNSYLVANIA*

Fooey and Adam were sipping the last of their Lambrusco. They were finished with dinner and they had several books, articles and papers filled with notes scattered over the table.

"So, what do you have? Let's sort of sum up where we are so far, OK?"

"Yep, but I have to tell you, I hope this so-called scientific approach helps, because it seems to go nowhere."

"Wait until we're finished, smarty-pants, and then we'll see. Go ahead, shoot!"

"OK. We've reviewed Tishman's texts and articles and we have only one thing and nothing else. Some radiation data and charts in Harry's log bear a remarkable similarity to one of Tishman's articles. Actually, it was one of his small articles while he was getting his doctorate in France."

"And we asked him about that when we saw him in Princeton, and I think he was a bit cagey and gave some flimsy excuses, don't you think?"

"I do, and he definitely wasn't free with his information."

"Like what?"

"Like, he gave us very little information about what was going on in '53 in Nevada, yet we know that most of that information has probably been declassified."

"But he did say that it was some paperwork about a trigger mechanism that was supposed to have been stolen."

---

147

"Yes, he did, but when pressed, he didn't say any more about it. I wonder where we can get more on that; on Nevada, I mean."

"Unh-hunh, you're right. Another thing I noticed, when you mentioned that we had seen two of his old frat brothers asking about Harry and Penn State and all, he didn't even ask who they were. He didn't show one bit of interest in the men or anything about Penn State."

"You're right. He also was very perfunctory about asking about my Mom, like it was an afterthought."

"Listen, Adam, I noticed that, too. If he was such an all-fired close friend and best man and everything, he sure as hell didn't show any warmth or great concern. Hell, how come he never followed up on keeping in touch with your Mom? Remember that your Mom told us that only a few people knew of her pregnancy and Tishman was one of them?"

"I do, and I thought that very strange. Do you think that there was some guilt showing there?"

"I don't know. What else do we have?"

"Tishman's eyes gave away some surprise when I told him that we had Harry's log, did you notice?"

"No. Uh, do you think there's something in there that could be more than we could discern?"

"God, we've spent a lot of time with that log and I don't know what else there is, do you?"

"Again, don't know, plain and simple."

"He sort of brushed off the 'DDT' reference, as if it was meaningless."

"Well, it just might be meaningless, unless the notes that Harry mentioned that had been left on his desk to see 'DDT' were some kind of set-up."

"Hey, show me the FAX from Carl in North Carolina about the pictographs you sent him."

"Here, this is very intriguing. Look at this configuration. This is the only thing that's of interest. See, here's a small evil face surrounded with these curly lines and between those lines Harry printed, very small, 'DDT'. And turn this one this way and between these little lines he wrote 'Spearson' You saw this when I photocopied them from the log."

"Carl says what about them?"

"He says that the symbol means beware of bad spirits in this location. Now, Harry put small question marks on both sides of the names, so it seems clear that he had some uncertainties or suspicions, what do you think?"

"That seems logical, but what was he suspicious about, eh? We don't know!"

"What did you make of Mickey Haws and his going on about conspiracy possibilities?"

"You mean about kidnapping or getting rid of someone by putting them in a plane and blowing it up?"

"Yes, and let's explore that for a moment. What if Harry found out something and he was going to let some important information out of the bag, you know, something really important. Wouldn't someone want to silence him?"

"By kidnapping him?"

"Or killing him."

"How? You mean blowing up a plane he was in? Why would someone have to blow it up? They were blowing up A-bombs, for cripes sake. They wouldn't have to do anything but get the plane or body close to a nuclear blast and the A-bomb would vaporize everything. Poof, like that! "

"My Mom did tell us a little bit about the work being done in Philadelphia and Desert Rock, and we know that drones were used out there."

"Could the radiation discrepancies he found be important enough to get him in trouble?"

"Who the hell knows? I don't know, but I guess it could have."

"Well, who would profit from a secret like that?"

The press and public would attack the government program, and maybe their work could have been curtailed or even stopped. That could be one reason."

"Even Tishman admitted that some of what Harry thought early on in the program proved to be fairly accurate."

"What about the things I brought home with me from Mickey's place? And what if that piece of bone is a human bone? We could get some DNA tests on it for the hell of it, and see if it matched."

"Matched who? You? You really think that there's a possibility that the bone came from Harry?"

"I, mmm, oh, hell, I don't know."

"I can tell you now that the bone is very calcified, and unless there's some viable tissue present, we're not going to get anything in the way of DNA. I'll take the few pieces into the lab and have a few pals take a look at the metal and the gold-colored stuff."

"Mickey said it tested as gold."

"I know, you told me, but if the metal is from a plane isn't it likely that some of the contact points, you know, the electrical contacts, weren't they coated with gold for better conduction?"

"I believe that's correct now, but I don't know about then, but have someone take a look."

"OK. What else do we have?"

"We've got two old frat brothers, Haws out in Nevada and even Tishman, all saying that Harry was a swell guy. Of course, my Mom says so, too, but that would be natural. We also have all of those people saying pretty much that Tishman was all right, but! Always the big 'but'. He was, by all accounts, not a trustworthy guy."

"And we didn't like him, either."

"Right!, but listen, just because he wasn't a sweetheart, doesn't mean that he's guilty of anything."

"You're right, Adam. Hey, are you OK?"

"Foo, I'm not liking the feeling I have that Harry might

have been kidnapped and killed. Do you think that's really a possibility? I mean, the rate we're going at this, part-time around our work and all, well, we start the new semester soon and we'll have even less time to work on this. It's frustrating as hell."

"For me, too, Adam. Let's consider getting some help."

"I thought the other day that maybe a professional, like a PI, might help us."

"A PI? An investigator? For real? Can we afford such a person?"

"I don't know, let's find out."

"Sounds like a good idea. Someone that knows what they're doing can get information faster and better than we can. The first thing we can find out is how to get in touch with some of the names in Harry's log."

"You mean, like, Spearson, Mitchell and the one pilot he got real friendly with, you know, Foley? Harry seemed to trust that guy and mentions him several times in the log, like he might have used him as a sounding board."

"Right. Look, I'll nose around and you make some calls and let's see what we can find. Hell, we spent part of our vacation money already, so we'll spend some more!"

### SEPTEMBER 8, 1992: PHILADELPHIA, PENNSYLVANIA

Adam was in the office of Francis A. Mulligan. Fooey had found out that an acquaintance from work, Erin McCue, was dating an ex-FBI agent and that he was now a private investigator with an office near City Hall. After discussing this contact with Adam, Fooey had her fellow worker get an appointment with Mulligan quickly. Adam had spent the first twenty minutes of their meeting telling Frank about his search for information about Harry, his disappearance and the frustration that Fooey and he experienced.

"We've spent a considerable amount of time on this and

a fair amount of our extra cash, but we seem to have come to a dead end."

"Listen, my friend, don't beat yourself up about it. Actually, for amateurs, even ones with doctorate degrees, you've done better than you realize."

"How so? We're at a loss and it's not as if we don't know which direction to go in, but we seem to have lost the whole damn compass."

"Look, Erin told me about you, and I know that you've been trying to do this part time. I also know that the new academic year just began and you probably feel overwhelmed. Listen, I'll dig around a bit, make some contacts with some of my FBI friends, and we'll start with you just covering my expenses. If we get into things on a heavier time basis, then we can talk about fees. Either way, I assure you that we won't break the bank. How's that?"

"That's great. Are you sure that's good for you?"

"Of course it is, otherwise I wouldn't have suggested it. I visit the labs where Erin and Fooey work, so I know what kind of people I'm dealing with. Let me ask you some questions about some of these notes and the log you have and, say, can I borrow those metal pieces you have there? I'll get those looked at in a real forensics lab."

"Absolutely, sure! Fooey took those to work and a colleague put them through some tests. She says that there is some trace of gold and the bone could be human, but she was right, the bone is so old, it can't be used for DNA testing."

"I'll get the work done as soon as I can, and I can get it done on the cuff."

"You're a good man to know. Oh, by the way, will you get me the whereabouts of the old Navy guys, Spearson, Mitchell and Foley?"

"That'll be easy enough. I'll call you in a few days."

Adam spent the next fifteen minutes answering questions and Frank took notes as they talked. He left Frank's office and headed toward Broad Street on his way back to the Medical School. He couldn't help feeling a bit excited and hopeful.

*SEPTEMBER 19, 1992: PHILADELPHIA, PENNSYLVANIA*

Adam was in the middle of a complicated statistical analysis, but the persistent ringing of the telephone on the wall in his lab scrambled his thoughts. He threw his pencil on the lab counter and picked up the phone.

"Adam, this is Mulligan. I've some information for you. Some of my inquiries are paying off."

"Hey, that's great. What do you have?"

"I've got the whereabouts of Mitchell, Spearson and Foley for you. Foley is in Florida and the other two are in California."

"Where in California? I've got a seminar in Santa Barbara coming up soon and maybe I can get to see those guys."

"Well, let's see. Spearson is in the Ventura County area and Mitchell is in a development in Port Hueneme. Both are close to a Naval Station at Point Mugu. My map, here, shows that to be about fifty miles south of Santa Barbara."

"Wonderful. Where's Foley?"

"He's a retired commercial pilot. I think he recently left American Airlines. He's in a place called Conch Key."

"Where's that?"

"In the Florida Keys, very close to Marathon. I checked and there's a small airport there at Marathon, if you want to get there."

"I think I'll try the phone first and then see if a trip is worthwhile. You know, our expenses are growing and Fooey and I would dearly like to get some skiing in this year."

"I understand that. OK, listen, I've got something else for you."

"Good. What else?"

"I don't want you to get excited about this, because much of what I do leads nowhere and often what sounds like a great bit of information turns into nothing. So, take my advice and keep cool and just simply follow the lead."

"You certainly have my attention. Tell me."

"Your father's Social Security number is active and in use."

"Wha?"

"No, no, listen to me. It's just a lead. The man's name is not Harry Connors. His name is Henry Shortledge. He's a couple years younger, but the SS number is the same."

"Do you think that it could be . . ."

"Adam, I told you, it has to be checked out. Let's be realistic here now, someone trying to hide himself wouldn't use his Social Security number, would you think? "

"Of course, you're right, but what do I do now?"

"See if you can get to the two men in California when you're out there, and talk to the pilot guy in Florida, and think about getting to see the guy with the same number. Oh, by the way, he's in Montana."

"Montana! Hell! Wait, maybe I can see him on my way back from the seminar in California."

"Whatever. You think about it and I'll FAX you the information about everyone, the addresses and everything, OK? Then I'll be talking to one of my pals in the Bureau today or tomorrow. He'll put me in touch with a guy who headed the investigation in Nevada in '53. He's a Deputy Director now. You go ahead with getting what you can from these leads and I'll get back to you as soon as I have something, OK?"

"Sure, and thanks very much. I think I feel better about these open doors, I just can't imagine where they all lead to."

"Adam, it's easy. It'll lead where it leads. You're committed to the search, and it seems to me that you're on the right path. Let me know what you find out and I'll be in touch."

*OCTOBER 20, 1992: LOS ANGELES, CALIFORNIA*

Adam and Fooey had just arrived at LAX on a non-stop flight from Philadelphia at around noon. They were headed for the car-rental lot. Adam's excitement about attending the conference and the paper he was presenting was compounded several times over at the prospect of seeing Spearson and Mitchell. During the flight, Adam had told Fooey about the long phone conversation he had with Bert Foley the evening before the flight. It was clear to Adam that Foley had been close to Harry during the time they had spent in Philadelphia and Nevada. As Harry's log had hinted, Harry had confided in Foley and told him several times about his fears concerning the radiation levels and what he considered to be irregularities in the reporting of those levels. Foley had been clear that he had reported his conversations with the investigators after Harry's disappearance.

Foley also recalled that he had the strong impression that the investigators with whom he spoke had felt that the radiation 'story' could have been a convenient front for Harry's plan to obtain the trigger mechanism details. Foley offered his own opinion without any prompting from Adam and that was simply that Harry was a good guy, married to a wonderful woman, an excellent, ardent and dedicated worker and a man that had absolutely no reason to be a thief and a traitor. He went on to say that he had thought that Harry was the kind of guy who could have been duped into some kind of trap and because he was making a stink he could have been kidnapped and killed, somehow, to cast suspicion on him. Foley said that he had reported his opinions to the investigators at the time. At the close of the conversation, he told Adam to call him at any time if need be.

Adam and Fooey had also talked about their decision not to call Spearson and Mitchell ahead of time, in the hope of gaining some advantage of surprise. They had decided to stop at Point Mugu on their way to Santa Barbara. With the car-rental map in hand, Fooey directed Adam onto the airport road and found the entrance to 405 north. Traffic was heavy and Adam preferred to remain quiet as he negotiated the unfamiliar freeway traffic and congestion. They found the Ventura Freeway exit and followed the big arrow towards Santa Barbara.

Adam relaxed a bit and his shoulders moved down to their normal place as the traffic eased off. A short time later, the 'Pt. Mugu Naval Air Warfare Center' sign directed them to Las Posas Road and what seemed like miles of strawberry fields. At the main gate, the guard pointed them to the security office, where they were refused visitor passes. Adam asked for the base phone directory and he dialed the number for the VX"4 detachment. Adam spoke to the duty officer, an Ensign Foulkes, and told him about his father's connection to the VX-4 and that he was trying to contact some of the personnel from the 1953 operation. Foulkes indicated that he could not help them regarding entrance to the base. He was helpful, however, in telling Adam that many of the VX-4 Group that retired and stayed in the area, had an active alumni association headed by a retired Navy Captain who hung out at the Wagon Wheel Motel nearby. When asked the name of the Captain, the Ensign reported that it was a Captain Spearson, and he was usually found at the Piano Bar at the motel. Adam got the directions to the motel, thanked Foulkes and left the security office with a smile.

In the car, Adam and Fooey decided that they would return to the motel after dinner and, since it was late afternoon, they could find Port Hueneme and, perhaps, Mitchell. When they got there, they stopped for gas, a drink and a pit stop, along with directions to what they found out was a trailer park with many retired Navy people living there.

Fifteen minutes later, they were in front of a 1960-style Airstream, well maintained and polished. Knocks on the door went unanswered and the two of them walked around the outside, peering and tapping the windows. A rather buxom woman with strawberry dyed hair and in a loose housedress came around from the rear. She had probably seen her sixtieth birthday quite a while back and a cigarillo hung from the corner of her mouth.

"Wadda ye want pokin' around here?"

"We're looking for Mr. Mitchell."

"There ain't no 'Mr.' Mitchell livin' around here. Now, if you're lookin' for Dutch Mitchell, now that's another story. It ain't goin' to do you much good, though, he ain't here and we're not 'spectin' him for a while. He's in a VA hospital somewhere."

"I wonder if we can leave him a note? Do you have his phone number, by any chance?"

"No, I ain't, he don't have a phone in there. He uses the office phone when he needs to and just slide the note in under his door, and I'll tell 'im that two Hollywood types was lookin' for 'im and they left 'im a note."

Trying not to break out in laughter, Adam got paper and pen from Fooey and wrote the note.

> Dear Mr. Mitchell,
>
> My name is Adam Kirkendahl and my father was Harry Connors. I'm trying to find out all I can about my dad, and I understand that you worked with him back in '53. If you remember him and have any information that would assist me, I would appreciate your contacting me at the following address, or calling me at the following numbers, collect. I'll be in Santa Barbara for a couple of days, after that, please call the Philadelphia number.
>
> Many thanks for anything you can do.

Adam glanced at his watch as he and Fooey got back in the car, and said,

"Listen, Hon, it's a quarter to four. What say we go to

Santa Barbara, check in, wash up, and then come back for dinner in the area to find Spearson?"

"Sounds like a plan, lover. Let's do it."

Adam found the entrance to the 101 and headed for Santa Barbara.

* * * * *

At about seven that evening they returned to the Ventura area. Reading the directions given to Adam by Ensign Foulkes, Fooey directed Adam to exit on Wagon Wheel Road. They followed the road around until they arrived at a low western-looking structure and parked in front. They entered the restaurant and looked around. A large piano bar area was to the right and the eating area in a large room to the left. They were seated in the dining room and, after a drink, they decided on mushroom steak, mashed potatoes and broccoli spears. The dinner was served on a sizzling hot metal plate, which sat on a cutout wooden base. They thoroughly enjoyed the meal and at about nine-thirty they moved to the piano bar and ordered a drink. The bartender seemed friendly, and Adam asked him if he knew of a retired Navy Captain by the name of Spearson. Smiling, the bartender pointed to the end of a bar where an older man smoking a cigar was seated next to a blonde.

"If you mean Puffy, that's him over there."

In the years since 1953, Spearson had aged quite well. Although slightly bald, he had no paunch, and seemed quite fit. Adam and Fooey got up from their stools and walked over to Spearson.

"Excuse me, sir, my name is Adam Kirkendahl, and this is my friend, Fooey."

With that, Spearson burst into laughter.

"Did you hear that, sweetheart; her name is Phooey . . .

now what kind of friggin' name is that? I thought I heard them all, but this one tops the list."

When Spearson quieted down, Adam explained the origin of the name, and Fooey contributed the fact that she was used to being ribbed and not to worry. Adam told Spearson his story and of his need to find the truth about his father. Spearson turned to Adam and suggested that they sit at a table in the corner, away from the boisterous crowd.

"You wait here, sweetheart. We have to talk."

After the three of them were seated, Spearson continued.

"It's been a long time, but I remember Harry well. He was a hell of a nice guy, and everyone liked him. I don't know too much about what was taken, but I never believed that Harry was a Commie. Now that son of a bitch Tishman, there's a guy I would believe could do something dirty, but not Harry."

Spearson continued to delineate the virtues of Harry and his misgivings about Tishman. When Adam told him of the molten debris he had been given in Nevada and, although there was no evidence to the fact, his father could have been aboard the drone, Spearson went ballistic.

"Goddamn it, all these years I haven't been able to get out of my head that the operation was sabotaged, and now I'm convinced of it. Not only that, but that fucking Tishman had to have something to do with it. Excuse my language, but I'm pissed!"

Spearson went on to tell Adam the details of the operation, including the miscalibration, Tishman's changing parameters back and forth, and so on. After some moments of silence, Spearson continued,

"Maybe we're jumping the gun. So far, there's no hard evidence that a person was aboard the drone. Maybe we're getting ahead of ourselves here."

"Gold traces were found in the molten debris, also."

"It's still circumstantial, but too many coincidences start

to make me nervous. You know, you should get a hold of Dutch Mitchell. He was the last person to be at the drone before takeoff, and I think he still lives in the area."

"We tried, but he wasn't home. We left a note to contact us when he gets back. Tell me, was it physically possible for Harry to be aboard? Was there space and time?"

"Absolutely. Even though there was a dummy in the pilot's seat, the bay behind, where we kept the electronics, had plenty of room, and Dutch should have been there all the time, I think. But he could tell you more."

After a few more drinks, Adam and Fooey expressed their thanks and said their good-byes. They promised to keep Spearson apprised of their investigation, and he promised to think about the day Harry disappeared, to see if he could come up with additional information.

As Adam and Fooey drove back to Santa Barbara, they discussed the day's events. Adam was now even more convinced that his father had been killed and placed in the drone to hide the murder. But questions still lingered. Why was Harry killed in the first place. How did the killer know that the drone would be destroyed? The killer had to be part of the project to have that kind of access. The discussion led them to other possibilities.

"What if Spearson, who seems so friendly and open, is really one of the bad guys and all his talking merely tries to direct our thoughts to Tishman or someone else? You know, some sort of end run."

"Sure, that could be. But now we have this Dutch Mitchell who was, perhaps, the last person to close the drone. We don't know if he had anything to do with this, either. Maybe he'll call or write."

"Well, if he doesn't, you should try to call him."

"Right, I will. OK, so, after the conference I'll stop off to see the man in Montana, as planned. I only have a day and a half, so I'll be back home soon. In the meantime, you could set up a meeting with Mulligan and we can bring him up to date."

"OK, I'll do that. This has been a day, huh? I'm tired."

"Me, too. It's only a few more minutes to Santa Barbara."

*OCTOBER 24, 1992: KALISPELL, MONTANA*

The flights from L.A., with a change in Denver, seemed amazingly short. Adam was deep into himself, wondering if he would find anything and whether this jaunt would be a waste of time and money. Actually, he had dozed off for more than half the trip and was making little noises when the announcement came to get the seats back in their upright position. He didn't notice the nice-looking lady across the aisle smiling at him because she thought he and his mild snorts were cute.

The chilly air outside the small terminal at the Kalispell/Whitefish Airport shook him fully awake as he made his way the few short steps to the holding area for the car rentals. He realized that this was one hell of an advantage over the huge airports he was used to. Waiting for a car-rental van to take you three miles to their car-park had always been a pain; and he had forgotten just how many stars you could see when you were in Montana.

The dashboard clock read 8:09 PM when he pulled onto route 2, northbound toward Martin City. It didn't take long to get to Hungry Horse, and he thought that he might stop and get something to eat before it got too late, but he was too hyped-up and had passed the little town before he realized it was behind him.

Adam had spent the better part of a summer out here during college. He wished that this trip could mirror his last journey. He had traveled out with three others to camp and fish and float the Flathead River. They had hiked out of Poleridge on the west shore of the river's north fork to a wild

161

and primitive campsite in Glacier National Park. After spending several days, they got back to their Volkswagen van and went down to West Glacier and hired a boat, took it way up the middle fork and white-watered all the way back. He sighed and smiled at how marvelous it had been.

The Martin City sign, quickly followed by a motel's dim lights, urged Adam to touch the brakes and coast into the nearly deserted lot in front of the only lighted window. The place didn't seem very inviting, but it didn't seem likely that there would be another place nearby. He knew that the next place would be West Glacier, about 6 or 7 miles up the highway. He wanted to be close to the Trading Outfit and as he got out of the car he noticed the place within spitting distance, directly to the north. Happily, the room was only thirty dollars. He asked the woman who owned the place where he could get some dinner and she pointed up the road.

"Tuesday nights ain't too lively here and, come to think on it, there ain't any nights that are too lively, but the saloon up there can fix you up with something. Tell Karen up there that you're staying with Martha down here . . . she'll take good care of you."

Adam dropped his small bag in the room and headed, on foot, toward the Packers Roost. Nearing the place he noticed that their lot was half-filled with pick-ups and cars and he heard what sounded like a hell of a crowd. In the Roost he, indeed, found a good-sized crowd, all with drinks in their hands, yelling and screaming and laughing around a very well-lit area toward the back of the place. Adam went to the pretty barkeep and saw the homemade banner over the bar that made him smile. The smile came all the way up from somewhere, through the worry, through the tired and through the hungry. The sign read, 'CHICKEN SHIT CONTEST'.

"Gimme a beer, please, and tell me what's going on back there."

Karen smiled, pulled the beer out of the tap, clunked it on the bar and pushed her face over the bar to get close.

"Tuesdays used to be dead here, so my partner and I took an idea we had seen somewhere and started the contest. We run it three or four times a night. We get these big sheets of heavy paper and make a checkerboard of fifty squares. Each square numbered, 1 to 50."

"And?"

"Yeah, so, everybody puts a dollar on a number here at the bar and then we get this chicken, see, and we put the big paper on that big plank of plywood and then everybody gathers 'round."

"I think I'm beginning to get the gist of the game, here."

Karen smiles and takes a gulp of her beer from a small bar glass.

"You got to go back and see. Take your beer and watch all the local yutzes make asses out of themselves urging the dumb bird to crap on their number. We even sell birdseed over the bar, so they can put some down on the playing field."

"The birdseed goes on their number to draw the chicken there?"

"At first that's what new folks do, but we all found out that the bird gets to your seeds, but craps in the next guy's block. The blocks, you'll see, are smaller than the bird!"

Adam was delighted with Karen, her slight Canadian accent, and the Roost.

"Sounds like a lot of fun. Can you get me something from the kitchen? Anything will do—burger and fries, chicken, anything, and please draw me another beer."

"Wow, not too many folks here say 'please' twice in ten minutes. Sure, I'll get you a platter. You go on to the back and I'll yell when it's ready."

Adam walked, but he thought he moseyed, to where the excitement was, and noticed what looked like a judge in a

ALTS

rooster mask calling for order as he held the bird above the platform. The blocks of numbers had been decorated by the bettors with magic markers, crayons, little stuck-on animal figures and seeds. One block even had what was left over from a freshly munched-on chicken thigh. It only took about ten or twelve minutes before the contest was over and the damn bird made a mess on the line between '22' and '23'. He saw, immediately, the rationale for the presence of a judge. Adam was much more relaxed when Karen called to him and pointed to his plate and beer on the bar.

"So, some lucky person wins 50 bucks. Can you bet more than a dollar?"

"Sure, but you have to put just one buck on each number you want. See, Montana law doesn't allow more than 50 dollars betting at a time, otherwise they call the place a gambling hall and that's illegal."

"The chicken is a rooster, right?"

"Right. He's Rudy, the Packers Rooster. It's tough to get a chicken to strut around. One week, my partner and I couldn't find a chicken to use, so she tried one of those small pigs. Ugh! Was that ever a disaster! That sonofabitch splattered three of my best customers."

A bit later, Adam walked back to the motel, not hungry any more and real pleased that he had some time not to think about anything important, or what tomorrow might bring.

### OCTOBER 25, 1992: MARTIN CITY, MONTANA

The rumble of trucks and the cold room woke Adam. He was disoriented for a few seconds and the motel room seemed strange. He groped his way out of the too-soft bed and did a little dance on the cold floor. Shaving, he thought about the prospects of seeing a man with Harry's Social Security number. After Mulligan told him about the number, Fooey had suggested that Adam phone out to Montana. They agreed that the phone would be considerably cheaper and easier, but Adam was convinced that he had to see this man and talk to him or be forever curious.

After Adam had a doughnut and some coffee from a small urn in the motel lobby, he pulled his collar close against the wind and walked across the highway to the Trading Outfit. The bell attached to the front door jingled lamely as he entered. A middle-aged woman, dark complexioned, smiled.

"Mornin', you're in early. Can I get somethin' for you?"

"I'm looking for Mr. Shortledge. Is he here?"

"Oh, yeah, Harry lives in the back. He's here all the time."

Adam felt his heart thump, beating faster, and he felt a strange sinking feeling in his chest.

"Harry? I thought his name was Henry."

"Oh, it is, but he uses his middle name. He's H.H. Shortledge. Wait a minute, I'll go get him."

Adam's pulse was fast and he tried not to panic, but felt himself sweating. He glanced around at all the pots and rugs and baskets, trying to calm himself. From the rear he saw a short, balding, very heavy man waddling toward him.

"Hello there, young man, what can I do for you? You can depend on us to offer dollops, drops and dabs of delectable items out of the west."

Adam's immediate reaction to this man was one of relief. He couldn't imagine him as Harry. He bore no resemblance to himself and was a good seven inches shorter and twenty inches wider. Adam kept things simple by merely telling the man that he was searching for someone and a Social Security search had come up with Shortledge's name. Adam assured him that he was not an official of any kind and showed him Harry's number.

"Oh, hell and be damned, my friend. I've been having problems with that mix-up for years. Look here, your last four numbers are 6969. I put in for disability two decades ago and they got my number fouled up. Why, damn if I don't get my check with the wrong number on it. I tried to tell them with letters but I gave up. Shoot! The amount's right and the bank puts it into my account, so I figured the hell with it."

Adam had noticed the birth date on the ID and it would seem that the owner of the Trading Outfit was fifty-six and Harry would have been sixty or sixty-one. The sinking feeling Adam had been experiencing was gone by now, but he was aware that replacing it was disappointment. It would have been easy to have finished with this once and for all.

"Mr. Shortledge, I appreciate your time. Do you mind a few questions?"

"Nope, not at all."

"Were you born and raised out here and did you ever go to Penn State?"

"I was born in Indiana, and my folks moved out here when I was in grade school. My dad was a railroad man here until he retired. Both my folks are dead now. And Penn State you say? Nah, I spent two years down in Missoula at the college, but it wasn't for me. I got into collectin' and buyin' and sellin' these goods. Nup! Never been east, don't like the sound of it anyway, but I wouldn't mind seeing all those things in the Smithsonian, you know the Native American collections."

Adam nodded, smiled and backed toward the door.

"Thanks again, sir, I'll get going now and I appreciate your giving me some of your time."

Adam felt warmer as he went back to the motel. The sun was heating up the macadam on the highway and he walked through a little bit of steam rising from it. He settled up his bill and drove back the way he had come the night before.

*NOVEMBER 5, 1992: WASHINGTON, D.C.*

Adam sat and fidgeted in the outer office of Tom Chapman, the Assistant Deputy Director of the FBI. After Adam's return from Montana, he and Frank Mulligan had met to exchange information. During that meeting, Mulligan had informed Adam that Tom Chapman had agreed to meet with Adam, and Mulligan took the liberty of agreeing to whatever time and date convenient for Chapman. Adam readily agreed to go to the Capitol for the meeting. He was very excited to hear, that Chapman had been the field agent in charge of the Nevada investigation in 1953. Mulligan had reported that Chapman's interest was piqued by Adam's quest. A buzz sounded at the receptionist's desk and a moment later, Adam was ushered into the large office. Chapman rose from a formidable-sized desk and they shook hands, after which Adam was invited to sit in a large upholstered chair.

"I'm meeting with you briefly today because I've known Frank Mulligan since he came into the Bureau and he's one hell of a forceful guy when he wants to be. He's never asked me for a damn thing in the past and he said I'd be intrigued by your visit. To bring you up to speed, Frank has informed me, by FAX, about all the inquiries and visits you've made, the results of some forensic tests made of metal, bone and gold traces. I also reviewed the photocopied log. Frank has been very efficient. He even physically dismantled the log, cloth cover, cardboard liner . . . everything."

"It's obvious that my mother and I feel strongly that my father could not have stolen documents or whatever. Everyone we've talked to paints him red, white and blue, and a Boy Scout to boot. Finding his log is, we think, at least some evidence of his concern and some of his suspicions."

"I can tell you this. I interviewed your mother in 1953 and we even gave her a lie-detector test, and I was convinced that she was truthful. She was, it was assumed, unaware of the activities of her husband. I didn't like finding out that we had missed finding the logbook. I admit to you that, at the time, I felt that there was something not quite right about the results of the investigation and there are several circumstantial elements. By the way, the metal fragments match our old data regarding the drone, and the gold traces are generally consistent with the type of gold used in inexpensive rings and the bone fragment could have been human."

"Could have been?"

"The specimen was reported to have been devoid of any viable material for definitive description. The fragment was exposed to tremendous heat and pressure, which compromised the cellular composition."

"Anything else?"

"Yes. Since most of the investigation has been downgraded, I can tell you that most of the metal found, some with the help of that Haws fellow, was from the drone—and the metal debris was found in an area consistent with the flight pattern and the blast force direction. Small charred cloth fragments of what was assumed to be the dummy material was also found during the analysis of the debris. Connors was the only suspect at the close of the investigation."

"But what didn't sit right with you?"

"Two days ago, I had the old file retrieved and I looked through it again. All circumstantial! The Bureau's theory was, simply, with so many things pointing to Connors it had to be him."

"Things?"

"Yes. The primary items are: one, at a known drop point— a local cleaning establishment in Las Vegas—several pictures show a man that fits Connors' description meeting with another man. Two, Connors, at least a couple of times, looks through another person's desk, and this other person is the one that had the trigger-plan copies. Three, a corner piece of that copy is found where Connors worked. Four, his complaints about the radiation problems were deemed to have been a cover for the real purpose of the theft of the trigger plan, and . . . five, he disappears into thin air. Before several hours passed, we had the usual exit cities on both coasts and the Canadian and Mexican borders alerted and there was never a trace. This usually means that there was a very efficient plan for an expeditious departure and the best way to do that was a fast private flight to the U.S. side of the Mexican border and a simple walk through an easy exit south. The FAA reported two flights early that morning from different private fields within 125 miles of the detonation site. Also, no passport exists in Connors' name. Interviews done at the two private airfields yielded no significant information. The planes or the pilots couldn't be found, for the planes were not locally berthed."

"As you said, certainly damning information, but not a fact in the lot. I mean, an actual piece of information that absolutely tags Harry."

"And that's what bothers me. It did then, and it does now."

"Why did you sign off on it, then?"

"We were ordered to handle this as a missing person case, not a spy case. Realize that, then, the work going on here was very hush-hush. I guessed that Washington didn't want to alert the bad guys that we were on to them so we didn't spook them into faster action and escape. It seems that it didn't work."

"Can you help us in any way? We could use your input and your advice."

"I'll tell you what. I've got exactly two months before my retirement and, as far as the office is concerned, your situation is the only itch left in my pants. So, I can't reopen this case officially, but I will look into it. I want you to know that Mulligan stressed the notion that your father's absence could have been because he was killed and disposed of in the drone or some other way. That would certainly explain things, but that conclusion would take a giant leap and, at this time, I view that theory with great skepticism."

"I understand, sir. Thank you. I really appreciate it very much."

"I'll contact Frank Mulligan shortly, and perhaps we three can meet down here again."

"That would be fine, sir, anytime you wish."

Another handshake and Adam was on his way out of the office and into a hallway where the heels of his shoes played a rat-tat-tat on the marble floor leading to the elevators.

### DECEMBER 15, 1992: PHILADELPHIA, PENNSYLVANIA

Max and Oz were hunched over Oz's desk sorting through ten or twelve envelopes. They had begun to get returns from the Frat reunion invitations. As they separated the questionnaires and the checks, Oz told Max that he had talked with Adam Kirkendahl by phone the previous evening. Oz reported that he had informed Adam that he and Max were old Frat brothers of Harry's and related how the two of them had become intrigued by the disappearance. Oz was apologetic about his hope that he wasn't sticking his nose where it didn't belong and, to his delight, Adam was very warm and receptive, told Oz about his own frustrating search and was happy that they wished to be helpful. Adam proposed that he meet with them as soon as possible. He further suggested that they meet Frank Mulligan and Fooey at some point to coordinate their efforts.

"Oz, that's great news. I like the idea of this project and we can help the kid, particularly with your computer knowledge."

"This was my thinking also. I told Adam that we have lots of time and computer availability's and access to many resources and a lot of information."

"Like what?"

"I had a thought about using the Freedom of Information Act, and getting all we could about the Nevada atomic blasts and Adam gave me the name of the outfit that Harry and Tishman worked for."

"You mean they weren't military guys?"

"No, they were civilian employees of this Sandia Corporation, or something like that. I'll search it out and get what I can. Another thing that's weird is that Adam told me, confidentially, that Harry's disappearance was linked to the theft of a new trigger device and the investigation puts its finger on Harry as a spy or at least a paid guy who stole the thing, whatever it is. So, I'm going to look into that spy thing, also."

"This is getting more mysterious all the time, huh?"

"Sure it is. And this fellow, Mulligan, is an investigator who was a FBI agent and he told Adam that he hoped to have some additional information after the holidays."

"You'll tell me how I can help and when and were do we meet, Adam?"

"He's calling me soon and we'll probably meet in Center City."

"Good. Hey, we've got all the paperwork and the checks in the large envelope. Tell me how to address it and we can get out of here and get some lunch."

*DECEMBER 18, 1992: PHILADELPHIA, PENNSYLVANIA*

Adam left work and walked down Arch Street toward his apartment. As he passed some shops in Chinatown he became apprehensive. This was the second day in a row that he had experienced this strange feeling. He glanced behind him as he crossed Ninth Street and saw nothing out of the ordinary. But the feeling that he was being watched—and perhaps followed—persisted. His stride increased and he realized that he was almost jogging. He tried to shake off the feeling that he was uptight and maybe he and Fooey should take a long weekend somewhere to get away from everything. Work was hectic and the time and emotional energy of the Harry-search thing was getting to him.

Fooey gave Adam a big hug and kiss as he entered their home and all the tension and anxiety seemed to subside and he felt like himself again.

"Hey you, let me wash up and you grab a bottle of Chianti and we'll go to Guisseppe's for dinner."

"Hey you, yourself, that's cool with me. Hop to it, though, I'm starving."

Fifteen minutes later they entered the warm little place on Third Street and received the typical greeting from the boss as he spied them coming through the door.

"Dottore e Dottoressa, buena sera, come va?"

Kisses on both cheeks followed the greeting and a flourished seating as napkins were placed on laps, all while Guisseppe ordered the wine and the antipasti prepared and brought to the table. After a few moments of animated conversation the couple was left alone, leaning toward each other. They clinked their glasses and tasted the slightly sharp, pungent fruit of some hill in Tuscany.

"Foo, I know you'll think this is crazy, but I think I'm being followed or watched or something."

"What do you mean?"

"Well, for the past few days I've had this strange feeling. I never see anyone when I look around, but this feeling overwhelms me whenever I leave the lab. You know, when I leave the building. It was there when I walked home tonight."

"Adam, that's weird. You're not usually like that. I mean, you've never gotten weird like that."

"Oh, it's probably my imagination from all the work at the lab, the teaching schedule, plus the frustration of our investigation. I guess I ought to try to forget it."

172

"Listen, bub, this kinda stuff scares me. I told you, you're not the type to get like this. I think we should call Mulligan tonight and tell him about it. Let's see what he thinks."

"Dig into that salad and let's not get carried away. It's just a feeling and I'll admit that it's a little embarrassing. Let's forget it and eat."

The two of them, happily, got involved with their food and the conversation turned to things that made them smile and laugh. When they returned to the apartment, Fooey called Frank Mulligan anyway. Frank took the call seriously and listened without comment. When she was finished, Frank reassured her and told her that he would figure something to do to check things out. That night, as they brushed their teeth, Adam told Fooey that he felt better after the call to Frank. As they brushed, they bumped with their hips trying to jockey themselves into a better position to spit in the sink. Laughing, Fooey got a mouthful onto the back of Adam's hand and Adam laughed most of his onto the mirror.

### DECEMBER 1992: PHILADELPHIA, PENNSYLVANIA

Adam had arranged to meet Max and Oz at a small luncheonette near Hahnemann. The three of them formed an immediate bond and were soon in a long and sometimes funny conversation about Penn State days at the fraternity. It seemed that when Adam asked about Harry, this one question primed the pump of information stored up in the memories of Oz and Max. Adam resembled Harry so much that the two older men felt that they were with Harry and treated Adam as if they had been close friends. They regaled Adam with stories he had never heard before. Adam was very pleased that Oz and Max wanted to join his investigation.

"What kind of help do you think you can give me, guys?"

"Oz, here, is an ace with his computer and ..."

"Max, I can tell him. I'm not mute."

"OK, OK."

"I've accessed the Internet and got reams of printout on the atomic operation in Nevada, and the Scandia Company and . . ."

"It's Sandia."

"Oh, right, yeah. We accessed the Freedom of Information Act at the Navy Department, and the AEC, for any data that's available, and Max has retrieved information from the files at the newspaper about Operation Upshot. I've only touched the surface on the Internet and God knows what we could find. I'm even trying to get what's available on Russian espionage activities during that period."

"Wow, that's fantastic. I really do appreciate the time you're spending."

"That's nothing, don't worry about it. So, when do we meet with this Mulligan fellow?"

"I've called him and he'll call me back with a time and place. I told him I was meeting with you two and he suggested that he could use your help in baby-sitting me for a few days. He said it would be soon, if that's OK with you both."

"Sure it is. We're not the types that go to Florida or someplace in the winter. What with the baby-sitting? What's that about?"

"It's sort of silly, but a few days ago I had a weird feeling that I was being followed. We told Frank and he watched my back for a few days, he said, and nothing every came of it. I think he wants to see if you both could be helpful in some way."

"Sure! anything we can do, kid. By the way, how does your lady think we should proceed?" "Fooey suggested that we put all our information on the table in an orderly fashion, just like setting up and analyzing a research project. And we can all get a grasp of the picture to date."

"Boy, that Fooey of yours sounds like some organized lady."

"You got it! That's what happens when a compulsive gets a research Ph.D. She's not like that about everything, though . . . you should see her closet. Hey, don't let on that I mentioned that last part."

Max and Oz chuckled and they all agreed to gather whatever they had and prepare for their meeting.

\* \* \* \*

Frank Mulligan met with Max and Oz the next day. He explained that their assistance would avoid several days of his billing costs to Adam. They chatted for a bit and got to know each other. They superficially discussed what was going on and Frank then gave them a short course on tailing Adam. He reported that he was pretty sure that Adam was just a bit stressed out, but he had closely watched him for several days and nothing seemed amiss. Frank had the solemn promise from both of these men that they would follow his instructions to the letter. All agreed that this was not a game, but serious. They were never to be closer than a half a block away, they were to take long photo shots of the streets they were on and in both directions. Adam would contact them to let them know when he was going to and from work and any outside evening ventures were to be covered. They could use their car during the evenings, but they had to be on foot during the day. This activity would go on for at least three days. Each evening they would check in with Frank and inform him of the day's activities.

Three days and one evening, Max and Oz performed their duties admirably. The reports each evening were negative. The only high spot was Max's report that there were a lot of cute girls around the hospital and Medical School, but they were all a bit too young. Unbeknownst to all was the fact that Frank, on two or three occasions, and for a couple of hours each, had tailed the tailers just to make sure that everything was OK. He called off the project and informed Adam and Fooey that all was well. He was sure that Adam had been just a bit 'antsy'. Max and Oz felt good that they were able to help to keep Adam's costs down.

\* \* \* \* \* \*

Over the next few days Adam had talked with Max and Oz several times, in person and by phone. At their request they received a few more jobs to do from Adam. They were busy getting more information about the radiation data from the Nevada A-bomb shots and digging into more data about the investigation following Harry's disappearance, but were happy to take on more. Adam asked them to review the Harry's logbook, for he wanted a fresh examination of the contents.

"Listen, Max, maybe you guys can come up with something by reviewing my father's notes in the log and when I visited the FBI in Washington, Chapman talked about the forensics and..."

"Whoa, Adam, slow down a bit, you're racing here."

"Oh, I'm sorry, Max, I get carried away sometimes."

"It's OK, Kid, Now a little slower, please."

"The bone and metal fragments that I gave to the FBI showed the presence of gold traces and I'd like more on that."

"And what else?"

"There were burned cloth remnants found also. I want more there too."

"OK, and?"

"Chapman seemed to be earnest in his invitation to call him if we had anything else to ask him, I'll fax him a note to tell him that you guys may call on him."

"Good idea, Adam, I'll discuss these things with Oz and we'll see what we can do, OK?"

"Hey, You both are great. Thanks. Call me whenever you can."

"Will do, kid, see ya soon."

\* \* \* \* \*

Oz and Max visited the FBI headquarters in Washington, for Tom Chapman did not want any telephone discussions. He had advised them that a vis-à-vis meeting was best and he could see them the day after Christmas. Chapamn was cordial and very helpful, for he had pulled all of the old files and had them ready for their meeting. He was very willing to discuss anything, but he would not allow Max and Oz to copy any of the documents. He did allow Max to pencil a few notes from the documents. Chapman told them about the gold traces. He reported that, yes, gold was used in some electronic contacts, but the traces found in the debris in question was a bit more than the minuscule amounts used in electronics. They discussed and reviewed the reports about the drone and the dummy. Max, grinning, wrote quickly as they talked.

"Mr. Chapman, I notice that there are pictures attached to the report folder about the suspected drop site in Las Vegas, may we see them?"

"Of course. You can see that they are all rather dark, but the taller man was thought to be Harry. As we have mentioned, the shorter man is not known either."

"There seems to be two sets of the same photos here."

"That's correct. Gentleman, would you excuse me for a moment? Please relax, I'll be with you in one minute. I want to give my assistant instructions about a meeting I'm having this afternoon. I'll only be a moment."

At that, Chapman picked up all the folders except the second set of pictures and went out to his outer office.

"Oz, he left the photos here. Is this what I think it is?"

"I think so, Max. Grab them and shove them in your inside pocket."

"Oz, I'm too nervous to steal."

"We're only borrowing, Max."

"Oh, In that case . . ."

Chapman returned and the three men spent the next ten or fifteen minutes discussing a few other things. Shortly before noon, Chapman closed the meeting, for he had a lunch meeting with the Director and he couldn't be late.

Max and Oz thanked him and found their way out of the building

"Max, let's grab some lunch somewhere and after we can go to the Vietnam Memorial, would that be OK with you? Then we can grab a taxi to Union Station." "Sure, Oz, good idea ."

\* \* \* \* \*

A few days later, Oz and Max were pouring over photocopies of Harry's logbook.

Each page spread out over Max's desk represented 2 pages in the logbook. It seemed obvious that Adam had pressed the open logbook onto the surface of the photocopier to be efficient and save space.

"Oz, look at this."

"Wha?"

"Here, look. See how these two pages are when viewed as separate pages, everything seems normal."

"Right, I see it. These Indian signs on the right page line up with a one-line entry on the left page. These signs on the right seem to be about the 'DDT' initials and Spearson's name, but they also could be a continuation of the line on the left. It almost seems that he added the signs as an afterthought."

"Read the line aloud, would ya?"

"He's here & he's not supposed to be around here ... looking at me. The 'looking at me' is printed and the rest of the page is cursive."

"And the line seems to be not connected to anything above or below it."

"Can you get some idea of when it was written?"

"Nah, I looked, but the only thing you can tell for sure is that the note is only a few pages before the last entries. I guess that puts it in early April, 'cause the blast was mid-month.

"Cryptic to say the least, Huh?"

\* \* \* \* \*

"Max, you have that information that Frank got for us?"

"Oh yes, I do, I do!"

"What are you so happy about?"

"Along with some other stuff, Mulligan sends us a copy of enlistment records of some of the people on the project with Harry."

"And?"

"So I just got finished with some computer searches that Mulligan told me about and I also spent about twenty bucks in Phone calls, listen! Mitchell, the one they called 'Dutch', came from a small place called Kent Island, Maryland. It's on the Chesapeake Bay, Maybe about forty-five minutes east of Annapolis. The Navy records show that he enlisted at age 17 at the order of some county court. It seems that he got into some minor jam with the law and they gave him an out by giving him a choice, you know, the County lock-up or military service."

"I remember, Max, they used to do that in those days. So?"

"Ok, here it is. He was a minor and a family member had to sign him into the Navy.

It seems that a Isabel Garmish signed him in and she's listed as his sister. All the phone calls lead me to her; she's living in The Presbyterian home on the island. I call there and I give them some cock and bull story so they tell me that she's fine and dandy and pretty much has all her marbles. The nice lady at the place told me that this home is a retirement place and Isabel owned a bar/café on the island for over 50 years. Oz, I think we should go see her. It's not too far away and as long as there's no snow in the forecast; we should talk to her."

"I think you're right, Max. This is the guy that Adam and Fooey never got to talk to out in California. He never returned calls either. Let's go tomorrow."

\* \* \* \* \*

The next morning was a cold and sparklingly clear day. Checking again, snow was not in the immediate forecast and the two pals, bundled up in warm jackets, drove south toward the Delmarva Peninsula. Weekday traffic was minimal and they got to the island in under 3 hours. They were received pleasantly by the Assistant to the administrator of the retirement home and had a very pleasant hour-long visit with Mrs. Garmish. On the way back to Philadelphia, they were elated at what they had uncovered, for Isabel was one heck of a talkative woman. Mitchell had been in a bit of trouble due to a slight misappropriation of someone else's Buick sedan. The sister had signed him into the Navy, for their mother could not. She had some serious medical problem and was confined to a state institution. Isabel, never married, worked in a diner and did what she could to support their mother. The different last names came about because the brother and sister had different fathers. She recounted that Dutch was insistent that their mom not spend her time in a state place that smelled of urine. He didn't like the way she was treated, either. He swore that he would come up with the means to get her into a decent place. A few years afterwards, they were able to move her into what Isabel described, as a wonderful and beautiful facility near Johns Hopkins. The hospital was affiliated with the facility and supplied all the medical care. She adored her brother for paying for their mom's costly monthly bills. Max and Oz were stunned to hear that the weekly fees were almost a thousand dollars. Added to that were the rather heavy doctor's bills, drugs and expensive equipment costs. Driving northward toward Pennsylvania, the two of then figured that over the more than twenty years there had to be a little under 2 million dollars spent on the care for Mitchell's mother. Isabel added with pride that after her mother was moved to the new place, Dutch bought her the bar/café that she worked in. She reported that her brother was a silent partner and rarely came to see her, but she got a bank check every month like clockwork so she could pay the bills for their mother. The Bar never made too much money, but it kept a roof over her head all those years.

As Oz's oldsmobile sped past the Philadelphia National Airport heading for Center City, they both shook their heads, thinking how amazing that an enlisted man in the armed service could do so well all those years!

*JANUARY 10, 1993: PHILADELPHIA, PENNSYLVANIA*

Oz is doing his four-finger dance on the computer keyboard and every once in a while, concentrating intently on the screen, he unconsciously hums a favorite Erroll Garner tune. Max is finishing his reading of about twenty or so pages of printouts.

"So, Oz, what did you see on the pictures that we got off the desk at the FBI?" "I'll tell you in a minute. Did you read all that stuff?"

"Yes, Master, I did. Now you show me yours and I'll show you mine."

"Smart-ass! OK, here are the pictures. What do you see?"

"Hmm, let me see. I see 15 or 16 shots. It's nice you seem to have put them in order. I see, um, a man whose face is not very discernible. He's about my height from the looks

181

of the store window behind him; he's got long-ish hair and even though these are black and white, you can tell that the hair is fairly gray and so is his beard. His jacket looks sort of like an old flight jacket and he's got a scarf and his shoulders are up around his head like the coat is not warm enough."

"That's very good, shmendrick, I'm proud of your observations. Now tell me what you read and what you think. I read all that stuff and more over the last three days and I've given you what I think is the meat of the material. Then I'll show you something on the computer. I'm a genius!"

"What are you talking about?"

"Never mind, wait until you tell me."

"And you think I'm a pain? OK, let's see. The newspaper clippings I got pretty much confirm the information about the Nevada Upshot-Knothole program that you downloaded off the Internet. The dates you got of the shots are consistent with the log entries that Harry made. The release of the declassified Russian documents, what's it called?"

"The Venona papers."

"OK, the Venona papers are very important here, 'cause it gives us a sense of the Russian spy machine and how it functioned. It goes way back to the thirties, and reveals intricate data and copies of cables that were sent back and forth into the seventies. They include the Rosenbergs and that bunch and their connection to the KGB, and name some of the high-ranking Soviet officials. And one guy stands out . . . wait, OK here, it's Duplatoff . . "Dusplatov, Du'ess'platov! I circled it."

"All right already, whatever."

"Go on, please."

"Yes sir, professor. I noticed several times that the Russians make it a point that the radiation data coming from the states should not be divulged to the, let's see, here it is, 'the American press'. It appears clear that they liked the idea of the high radiation levels. They probably also liked the idea that hundreds of our buildings had harmful asbestos in them and lead in all the paint. Anyway, they refer to many projects, but you've circled a couple of more things."

"I circled the project that involved, like, the theft of something with a code name 'Helen'."

"And you circled the code name 'Paris', too. What's the connection?"

"See? All the time I told you that you took too many of those science courses when you should have taken more literature and art courses."

"I apologize, my esteemed Master, so what the hell are you saying. Tell me. Oy, the suspense . . ."

"It seems clear that 'Helen' was the code name for the trigger mechanism that was stolen at the same time that Harry went bye-bye. We have to believe that it's more than a coincidence that in the Iliad, the Trojan War started when Paris went to Sparta and snatched Helen up."

"Hey, watch your language! You never know when a kid could be listening. So you're saying that a Russian agent they coded as 'Paris' stole the trigger thing whose code name was 'Helen'?"

"Why not? What do you think of that? I dug that out of my great memory from the Greek mythology literature course."

"I think you're marvelous. It just proves that you definitely aren't up to the 'Z' in Alzheimer's—at least not yet. There were other notes about this somewhere that I just read. I'll have to dig around and find the connection. So what did you want to show me about the copies of the pictures that we borrowed?" "I got more about the spy thing, but that can wait until we get together with Adam and his group. Here, look over my shoulder while I play this on the screen. Tell me what you see. Look closely. I'll start it. Look!"

"Holy shit! It's the guy walking with the old jacket and the scarf walking from inside the store to the outside. Hey, that's too fast. Can you play that again, but slower?"

"Sure. Here it is at half speed. Tell me what you see."

"It's a little like Charlie Chaplin, but the guy seems to be walking and I'll be damned . . . the guy has a limp. Am I right?"

"Yep, that's what I see, too. You can't make out his face very well, but he has a damn limp, for sure."

"How in the hell did you do that?"

"I told you I was a genius. You scan each picture, in sequence, through that thing there and you save them on a clipboard. Then you paste them into an animation program. By playing with something called the image tab dialog, you can set the pictures up as frames for a continuous look, like a motion picture. The program can be adjusted to fill in the images in between the photos so it looks like action instead of a series of still shots."

"Amazing! I wonder if the cops or the FBI ever picked that up?"

"Who knows! I'm sure they could have done this in some primitive way back in the early fifties, but I don't know."

"Holy smokes. Wait 'til Adam sees this."

### JANUARY 14, 1993: PHILADELPHIA, PENNSYLVANIA

Oz places the book he's just finished on the desk and adds several notes to the three pages of scribbles on his lap. There's a little smirk on his face as he picks up the phone and dials Adam's number.

"Hello, Adam, this is Oz."

"Good morning, Oz. I'm sorry, I don't have a meeting time yet."

"That's OK, Adam. I didn't call for that. Whenever you set it up will be good for us. Max and I are coming up with some interesting things for us to think about."

"Mulligan is waiting for some information from his contact in Washington. He said that it might add some fresh info to our meeting. What do you have for me?"

"Last year, in July of '92, the National Security Agency declassified something called the 'Venona Project'. This project started in 1943 when the NSA broke the Soviet code and they started to translate and analyze thousands of encrypted cables. Would you believe they did all this manually, without computers? Anyway, we went over these Venona papers that I downloaded from the Internet, and there's a great deal of information there, but several things pop out at you, not the least of which is a name."

"Whose name?"

"A soviet high-ranking spy type person. His name is Anatoly Dusplatov."

"And?"

"Max and I were reviewing other Internet sources and came up with a recently published book, 'Confessions of a Russian KGB Officer'. The coincidence here is that the author is this Dusplatov guy. Apparently, he's still alive, and I asked Max to get a copy of the book from the main library, in town. I just finished the book and I made several notes to keep my thoughts on paper. Max read the thing also and we're going to compare notes shortly. Yesterday, before I started to go through the book, I accessed the New York Times book review section for several weeks after the publication date and I find a very lengthy review."

"Good going, Oz. You have a damn good way to dig out things. What did you come up with?"

"Well, among other things, he reveals special projects and tasks, as they were called, and he names and sometimes characterizes special agents and even double agents. One of the projects involved the U.S. Atomic Program, which included the period of time Harry was out in Nevada".

"Any names mentioned?"

"No and he gets pretty vague about it. He does allude to

one or two of his people being out there and the code name 'Paris' is used. Oh, yes, by the way, all of this book has to be taken with the usual grain of salt."

"Why's that?"

"The reviewer made several strong statements indicating that historians and other experts think that Dusplatov probably amplified his part in the KGB and the projects about which he wrote. It was strongly suggested that much of the intrigue and names in the book were fabricated. The Russian even indicated in the preface of his book that no notes were ever taken out of the building, for it was against the law. So his entire book is based on his memory."

"You'll tell us more about this at our meeting, right?"

"Of course. Max and I will review everything we have. Don't go away, though. I have a job for us to do."

"What do you have planned?"

"All this reading, you know, the Venona papers, the spy book, and I've got reams of other stuff, all of this is very compelling. So, I dig further and the book jacket, of course, tells me that Dusplatov lives in Brooklyn with his son. He's 83 years old and lectures at times around the city. I figure the lectures these days are for him to hype the book, so I call the publisher and find out that he has three dates set up in New York City, and here's the thing . . . he'll do a short reading, answer questions and autograph books right here in Philly!"

"Great! Do you think we could get to see him? Where will he be?"

"Whoa, whoa, calm down. I'll tell you, I promise. He'll be at the bookstore at Rittenhouse Square this Wednesday. I had Max call the publicist at the publisher's and he gave them a story that may have included some so-called producers that could be interested in a movie. This is not to be quoted, of course. Anyway, you, Max and I will meet the old spymaster and his agent in the square about twenty minutes before he does his book thing."

---

"That's fantastic—I can't wait. What do we say to the man's agent?"

"You let Max and me take care of that. We'll engage him in a very sincere discussion while you get to speak to the Russian. I'd like you to remember to ask him if there were more than one agent involved out there. The book said that there was always a control, you know, like in the spy novels, a person that was a local director."

"You both are great. You've opened up several new avenues that we would have never found and, of course, I'll ask him anything that you want me to."

"OK, OK, one other thing. Max and I couldn't help notice that there's a loose end in your attempt to see as many people as possible that knew Harry in Nevada. At least those who would, maybe, know something."

"Huh? What loose end?"

"We read the note file you gave us, and the copy of Harry's log, of course. And the man who was the Chief Petty Officer, this Dutch Mitchell . . . you never got to see him in California and he never called you."

"I did leave a note asking him to call me collect and I tried probably a dozen times to get him, but no one ever answered. I even called the operator to check on the line that was in the trailer park office and the line was in working order."

"Max and I feel that he should be found and we should get to him somehow."

"We?"

"Sure, why not? Look, you ask Mulligan to find out where he is. Your notes said that when you were out there, a lady told you he was in the VA hospital. So, find out and we'll go see him."

"I'll call Frank this afternoon and I'll get back to you as soon as we can set up our meeting."

"Good, you do that. Max is due to pick me up soon, so

you go and I'll wait for your call. Say hello to that pretty lady of yours."

*JANUARY 20, 1993: PHILADELPHIA, PENNSYLVANIA*

Anatoly Dusplatov sat on a bench in Rittenhouse Square, bundled in his heavy fur coat. His fur hat was of a different color and looked like Persian wool. His cheeks were rosy from the cold and he munched on a soft pretzel. He had been unknown for his entire career in Moscow, for he was only known by sight or name by very few. In the past several weeks, however, he had begun to enjoy a sense of notoriety due to the recent publishing of his book. At his age, he still couldn't rationalize the dichotomy of the American society. Even here, in this park, examples of this dichotomy were evident. He looked around this affluent neighborhood and he saw women in elegant attire wearing sneakers; a homeless man rummaging through a waste bin; a young woman pushing an expensive carriage and walking her dog at the same time; and a group of youths running and shouting, carrying, what was it called? Oh, yes, a 'bomb box'. How these people won the cold war, he could not comprehend. His agent, a man in his forties, but looking older with his white hair and an old Chesterfield overcoat, turned to Dusplatov.

"Are you warm enough?"

"Yes, of course. In Russia we have much colder than this. This is pleasant, to rest a bit before I talk in the bookstore. I enjoy this very much to see everything. Those boys that went by with the noise thing—it's called a 'bomb box', yes?"

"No, Anatoly. In America it is called a boom box."

"Ah, so no difference. 'Boom', 'bomb', no difference to me."

Adam, with Oz and Max, approached the bench with a little anxiety. After brief introductions, Oz requested that he and Max speak to the agent as they strolled a bit while the younger man talked with the author. Adam smiled as he sat next to the older man.

"Sir, I'm hoping that you can be helpful. While my friends talk business with your agent, I'd like to ask some questions. I'll be perfectly honest, I need information from you. My father's name is Harry Connors. I never knew him. In April of 1953, while working on A-bomb tests in Nevada, he disappeared. At the same time, plans for a new trigger device were stolen, and to make it short, my father was never found. It was thought after the formal investigation, that he was the person who took the plans. This devastated my mother and I feel that he was killed to keep him quiet." During Adam's entire story, the older man stared straight ahead, unblinking, chewing on the last bite of his pretzel.

"A most interesting tale. And you read in my book something about this?"

"Well, not specifically, but I believe there is some connection between the trigger device and the code name, 'Helen'. I have also reviewed much of the translated Venona papers, which I'm sure you're familiar with, and made some comparisons between those and some of your writings."

"Quite a detective you are, young man. You do this to get the father's name to be honored again?"

"Yes, something like that. My curiosity is one thing, but to ease my mother's life-long worry about this is my major concern."

"Ah, yes, a very honorable and noble activity. I commend you for that. What do you want of me?"

"Do you know Harry's name, Harry Conners?"

"No."

"You recall the code or cable name of 'Paris'?"

"I know the name 'Paris'. Why is that important?"

"Paris steals Helen and . . ."

"Ah, you know mythology. It's a good connection, but so **evident? Too simple a connection, yes?"**

"Were there agents of the KGB at the Nevada sites and was my father one of them? Do you remember if there was more than one agent there?"

"Young man, there could have been one or two. Perhaps there could have been ten."

"Several book reviewers were very strong in their opinion that the so-called facts in your book and even some of the names of agents and double agents were fictionalized for your own aggrandizement."

"An old Russian proverb for you: 'There will be trouble if a cobbler makes pies'."

"And that means what?"

"A man who reviews books should be concerned with his own work of telling if the book is good or bad, is written well, not give advice about things they know nothing about."

"So you're saying that the reviewers are not correct?"

"Mostly, I would say that."

"The Venona documents reveal that several operatives were at work in New Mexico, at the Atomic Labs, as early as the World War II forties, and that cables were sent to Las Vegas and routinely diverted through Mexico City. Your people were in both places and your book reveals names of some that spent time in Alamogordo, but no revelations about Nevada."

"You seem to have done some good homework."

" Are you familiar with the name Dr. Richard Tishman?"

"No."

"Chief Petty Officer Dutch Mitchell?"

"No."

"Navy commander Spearson?"

"No. Your time is wasting, because I don't know these people."

"The Venona papers indicate that a cable was sent that

involved the authorization to pay the second of three install-
ments in the amount of 150,000 dollars. The cable was dated
in February, 1953. The third and last payment was to be made
after the receipt of something referred to as 'Gelen'. Another
amount—I think it was 50,000 dollars—was to be dropped at
a usual, predetermined place. Doesn't this seem to imply that
there was more than one person involved? And isn't it true
that in the Cyrillic alphabet there is no 'h' and very often a
Russian would use a 'g' in its place?"

"You are indeed a very astute young man, but I know
nothing of this you speak."

"It is known that soon after early 1953 the Russian atomic
program shot forward very quickly and caught up with the
American program. Can you not tell me, please, was my father killed, and did someone other, like 'Paris', obtain the
trigger plan."

"In all good conscience, I can neither give nor not give
credence to such theories. Another Russian saying: 'A fly will
not enter a closed mouth'."

"You seem to be more interested in your proverbs than in
giving me some help."

"Young man, you are very intelligent and your diligence
is noteworthy, but when one grows older and can no longer
collect women, one collects proverbs."

Adam stood, thanked the old man for his time and started
toward Oz and Max, walking and talking on the other side of
the park.

*FEBRUARY 12, 1993: PHILADELPHIA, PENNSYLVANIA*

The day of the big meeting had arrived. Some snow remained
on the streets and it was one of those typical Philly winter
days: cold, dreary, very wet and no one really knew what to
do with the snow as it turned into blackened slush.

Fooey, Adam, Frank Mulligan, Oz and Max sat around

the kitchen table. All had a mug of coffee in front of them "The meeting was Fooey's idea, so I'll let her get to it."

"OK, thanks, Adam. We have a heck of a lot of information and I thought it would be a good idea to treat this just like a research project. We usually refer to something like this as an analysis forum—very informal. What we try to do is bring all of the data together and discuss all the parameters. This includes facts and inferences from all derived data. In research, we then summarize and then try to arrive at some logical conclusions. The latter is included in a summary when we publish the results. In this case, we'll try to also include hyperbole and hunches. An outline of major topics is used as a directional but not a limiting plan for our discussion. The first topic in my outline for discussion is 'the investigation'. I'd like Frank to start, please. Frank?"

"Over the last several weeks, Chapman at the FBI has given me a great deal of information. I forwarded some of it to Max and Oz. The investigation points to Harry, by default. He was the logical culprit, because he had looked through the desk of one of the people who had the trigger plans. A small piece of that plan was found in his abandoned car at the military facility. It was felt that his disappearance was too neat and it was clean as a whistle, leading to the conclusion that it was very well planned. Not a trace was ever found. The FBI rejected the theory that he was duped or killed and removed via the drone. They felt strongly that the destruction of the drone was intended to obscure the theft of the trigger plans—a diversion that's all. The FBI had pictures, not definitive mind you, but of a man matching Harry's description. Pictures taken at a known 'drop' point in a Las Vegas store during the time that he was there."

"Let's hold it there for a moment. Adam, you have something in the way of a rebuttal. Let's have that now, OK?"

"Sure. First of all, my mom has mentioned several times that Tishman was the same size as Harry and they often wore the other's clothes. The point being, that many people have the same general build. On the day of the blast, when he disappeared, the sentry logs show that no one went in or out that shouldn't be there, and Harry was never logged out. Harry's car was still where he had parked it. Surely, no proof that it was abandoned, as they put it. No trace of Harry on the base could indicate a cover-up, and not a so-called clean operation. Agent Chapman, himself, has mentioned several times that he always thought there was something funny— that is, wrong—with the results of the investigation. Admittedly a hunch, but there it is. Everyone, to a person—before, during and well after those years—swore that Harry was one hell of a good guy. A 100-percent consensus. The words used to describe him included 'trustworthy', 'honest', 'a fair guy' and 'a play-it-straight guy'. The investigation never came up with any money added to any accounts or any new ones opened, and there was never a passport issued. The two coasts and the Canadian and Mexican borders, all the exit points were alerted and, essentially, closed. Harry's log mentions some suspicions of Spearson and Tishman. Finally, and this was mentioned by several others before me, that he had no motive. He was newly married, he was a happy and content young man, never politically motivated and never a radical of any kind, even as a kid in college."

"Let's hold for a moment. Frank, you had a comment?"

"Yes, Adam. You mentioned that all the possible exits were alerted, but there were a couple of private flights, possibly from near Indian Springs."

"That's true, but the investigation never completely nailed down the facts about the flight plans and, as far as I'm concerned, there's no way they can prove anything. I also think that the discrepancies in the radiation reports were never taken seriously."

"At the time, Adam, the investigators thought that was a diversionary tactic."

"Right, but even Tishman owns up to the fact that there were radiation mistakes made back then. Hell, in Harry's log, he writes often that there were rarely any radiation tags used during many of the shots. Remember that he wrote that he had received a couple of notes to look on or in Tishman's desk and that could have been a set-up to make him look guilty."

"Those notes could have been made after the fact, too, Adam. And please remember that I'm just being the devil's advocate here."

"Oh, I know that, Frank. We promise not to kill any messengers here."

"Hah, I'm glad to hear that. Fooey, what's next?"

"Say, Max and Oz, you both have been very quiet."

"I think that we're absorbing here. Most of the things you're discussing are familiar to us. We'll wait until we have some of our stuff to contribute. OK with you, Max?"

"Sure, sure. One thing that we think is very important we can add here about what the FBI called a diversion. Oz and I feel strongly that this idea is just not logical."

"How so?"

"The plans were readily available to whoever took them. He, they, whoever, could have just taken them and gone away. Of course, a missing person would have been considered the guilty person. But, it was only some papers . . . no one had to disappear at all. Copies of the papers could easily have been taken out and delivered or sent to someone. We think that there was a diversion, but not as the FBI suspected. The diversion was to throw off the investigators. The papers are taken; someone disappears, he can't be found, so he must be the guilty person. Oz and I think alike on this. We think that this is another strong clue that Harry disappeared in the blowup of the drone."

"Hell, that seems damn logical to me too."

"All right then, let's continue with Spearson. What I have

in my notes, let's see—Spearson always seemed to have plenty of money and he was something of a womanizer. He was close to the situation, that is, proximal to the action, and he could have had something to do with the diversion or screw-up of the drone's flight pattern that drew it too close to the blast."

"Again, all circumstantial. Several people were close to the action, as you put it. Anything else?"

"Harry's log had the Indian sign that indicated that Harry was suspicious of Spearson. Adam told me once that his mom had told him that Spearson had hit on her several times when they were in Philadelphia at the naval base. She didn't like him very much."

"So, he was a creep, we can agree on that. Our visit to see him was relatively unproductive except that he had very positive things to say about Harry and very negative things to say about everyone else. Tishman, in particular. He acted like the real good sport, buddy-buddy type. You know, expensive cigars, informal, but very expensive clothes. Frank, what did you find out about Spearson?"

"Only the basics. Good record in the Navy. Before joining the VX-4 group and the Sandia people he spent six years in Navy intelligence. He retired with the usual promotion and the only thing that may not fit is his life-style. Well, actually, it's not quite over the edge, but maybe he plays it down a bit."

"And that is . . . ?"

"His home in California, I would say, is a bit pricey and so is his car, actually two of them. Not outlandish, but maybe he invested well."

"What about the cars and the house?"

"The tax records indicate that the house is worth about 650,000 dollars and he's got a Porsche sports car and one of those British land cruisers, both fairly expensive."

"Anything else?"

"That's about it. Chapman was helpful getting this info."

"Good. Oz, you had something?"

"Yes, about the Indian signs. Max and I examined the log closely. We had the photocopies and on each copy there are two pages of the log, side by side. Looking at each page by itself, the signs are connected to Spearson and Tishman, but looking at two pages side by side, is different. Harry had written a line in the middle of the first page, like, 'He's here again and he's not supposed to be around here'. Opposite this line, but on the next page, are the signs."

"What does it mean?"

"We don't know, but it must have been written in early April, a little bit before the blast. More important is what we think it may show."

"Show what?"

"It seems to show that there was someone or something else going on here. Perhaps Harry saw a person that turned out to be the real culprit and maybe this is another indication that there was more of a motive to get rid of him."

"Whew! this is getting complicated. Anything else?"

" Maybe we could get to Tishman. We knew him at college, as you know, and I've talked to him recently about an upcoming fraternity reunion."

"OK, let's move on to Tishman. Adam, you first."

"We have a universal story on him regarding his personality and integrity. Max and Oz, here, corroborate that he was a socially and politically active young man, but the women he took out, college friends and work friends found him to be less than forthcoming and an unreliable friend. He never married. He spoke well of Harry and felt that accusations against him were ludicrous, even though it was he that told investigators that Harry was overly curious about the trigger mechanism. Apparently, he lifted some of Harry's radiation work and used it in one or two professional articles which were published several years after Harry's disappearance, but when we saw him he admitted that using the materials was a mistake. He even went so far as to admit that there were, indeed, radiation reports that were in error and time proved Harry correct in that regard. Harry's log has the Indian sign for bad guy, or whatever, on Tishman, but we just learned that that might not be correct. The log also indicates that two messages were left on Harry's desk to get something from Tishman's desk. As I've mentioned before, this seems to be a possible set-up to me. The last thing I have is about the flight plan alteration of the drone. He and Spearson had an argument about this immediately before the blast. Some change was made, a slight alteration of some sort. Tishman wanted Spearson to abort, but he would not. There had been some name-calling."

"If Tishman was the guilty person, why would he have demanded the abortion of the detonation that morning?"

"Perhaps a show, a piece of theater for everyone's benefit? He knew Spearson's driving personality and ego so it would have been an odds-on bet that Spearson would order the go-ahead anyway."

"Yeah, true, but anything's possible. Oz?"

"I'd like to bring up the 'Paris' code name, OK?"

"Absolutely. Shoot!"

"Let me back up a bit. Max and I have reviewed several times all the data we could find on the Upshot-Knothole project and the Sandia Company, downloaded reams of spy stuff from the Internet. We even got the government to send us a two-inch thick computer printout of things I requested ala the Freedom of Information Act."

"Wow, that's terrific!"

"Anyway, sifting through all this stuff was intriguing and certainly educational. Radiation and fallout data indicates that Harry was right-on about the generally lower figures reported that were purposely misleading at the time. Even one of the

---

197

documents—let's see, number 3695—had figures that were taken off-site. Like, they found sheep thyroid levels were increased and so were infants as far away as Utah. There was even a claim by someone for a horse that died because of contamination, and the claim was paid.

We have several copies of reports and data indicating that the Russians wanted the radiation levels to remain high and probably contaminate as many people as possible. There's some logic to the idea that Harry could have been making too much noise about this. Max and I think that there's motive here. Well, I'm getting carried away. We found that the scientists had to check their logs into security after the logs were filled."

"What was that for?"

"Safe keeping, I imagine, and they were filed so they could be consulted at any time, but only in the presence of a security person. And here's the interesting part. Only two of Harry's logs were listed in safekeeping, when the others had four or five."

"OK, so what does this mean, so far?"

"We know that Tishman's gamma and neutron figures were wrong. This was either an error on his part or his actions were purposeful."

"Why would he do that on purpose?"

"If he was the 'baddy' in this—and our reports showed much radiation damage to a large section of the west—maybe it involved a plot to harm a good number of the American population and foul up the ranching and agricultural industries. I think, maybe, a plan to slow the American machine down. The cold war was a real war of sorts; we have to remember that."

"What about the possible missing notebooks?"

"Harry hid one of his logbooks, the one that was found. The others could have had information in them that may have pointed more directly to someone . . . . someone that could have arranged Harry's death and maybe took the other logs."

"Mmm, could be. Oz, go on, please."

"One other point about the printout from the government. There was an inventory of equipment—gear, spare parts, what-have-you—that Sandia and the Navy had that went out to Nevada at the time of the project and that came back to Sandia when it was over. Of course, all the planes and the Navy things went back to California. They listed three drones that were moved from the Naval Base here in Philly, and two that were sent back to Sandia in New Mexico for some kind of refurbishment. This makes sense, because one was lost when the drone was destroyed."

"Right, and we know from the investigation report that cloth remnants were found by Mickey Haws, the digger friend of Harry's out in Nevada."

"So, we also know that there was room in back of the dummy in the drone for a body to be stashed. We also didn't pick up on the little note about the fabric, that it was a cloth material, but couldn't be tied absolutely to the dummy. It was almost unidentifiable because of the blast heat. It could have been part of someone's clothing."

"Yep, this adds more fuel to my feeling that my father was in the drone and destroyed."

"Max, tell the group about some of the notes you took when we saw Chapman in Washington."

"The forensics report that the FBI has includes the fact that the remnants found in the debris thought to be from the drone include very little burned cloth remnants. They also found the charred remnants of what appeared to be a square, thick piece of leather. The examiner said that it was consistent in size and roughly the shape of a heel from a leather shoe. We checked with Foley, the pilot pal of Harry's, by phone, 'cause we wanted first hand info if we could get it. I asked him about the interior of the drone, like was cloth and or leather used in the cockpit. He said no, only a bit of soft plastic over a thin padding on the metal seats in the cockpit. No upholstery, no leather, no nothin'. I asked him about the space behind the seats in the cockpit and he said there was plenty of space to stash a full grown adult."

"Tell them what else you found, Max."

"Navy records and Harry's log indicates that the dummy on that shot was plastic and unclothed. Harry seemed to have remembered that a bunch of them got bawled out in Philly for doing something funny with the dummy. Some bigshot gave them hell, so they never did anything like that again. Harry had a very brief memo to himself in the log about this."

"Mickey Haws find of the metal piece with some bone and traces of gold could point to the use of the drone to get rid of Harry, even though the bone was not 100 percent identifiable as human and the trace of gold couldn't be identified either?"

"Oz, didn't Chapman tell us that the gold found was the kind that was used in inexpensive rings?"

"Right, Max."

"I agree that it's completely circumstantial, and we have uttered this word many times, but when the circumstances continually point in the same direction, we've got to sit up and take notice."

"Hey remember, that's exactly how this whole mess was pinned on Harry!"

"Oh yes, you're right about that."

"Oz, what else?"

"Let me go on to the Venona papers and the book that this Dusplatov wrote. We know that the Russians had spies in the U.S. for years. We probably had the same over there. Who knows? Dusplatov's name comes up several times as a bigwig in the KGB. 'Paris' was the code name for either a person or several persons as a group operating in and around the Nevada project. We can assume that the code name

'Helen' was used for the trigger device. We told Adam of this because we believe, as in mythology, that the logic is there that 'Paris' stole 'Helen'."

"But that's so damn obvious. Were they that naïve or just plain stupid?"

"Fooey, you're right, but people like that probably like to have some fun with names, or yes, they're just stupid. For example, these same Venona documents reveal that many cables were sent, typically via Mexico, back and forth to the Rosenbergs or about the Rosenbergs. You know, the famous spy case that was all over the newspapers thirty years ago. Anyway, in one cable sent relative to some cash that was needed to continue their work, the Russians made the glaring error of referring to Mrs. Rosenberg as 'Ethel', her real first name, instead of her code name! Another simple case of a very evident name was about a man named 'Morros' who wrote a book in 1959 about being a counterspy. The Russians gave him a cover name of 'Frost'. And the reason was that the Russian word for frost is 'Moroz'. Now how putzy could they get? So, yes, they could very well have put 'Paris' and 'Helen' together, very much so. Max and I talked about this and he came up with the fact that the 'Helen' was written as 'Gelen' because there is no 'h' in Russian. We told Adam this and he confronted Dusplatov with it—and more—but couldn't get anything from the old Communist. We'll get back to him in a minute. The 'Paris' thing was bugging me until we put together from our old fraternity boys, and Tishman himself, that Tishman spent two separate periods in Paris. Once for an exchange semester as an undergraduate, and another time in graduate school. He got his master's degree there."

"That's a pretty slim connection, isn't it?"

"Yes, it is, but the Venona papers give us detailed accounts of how the KGB recruited young, impressionable college kids, mostly while they were in major cities in Europe. Guess which was their most successful and productive recruiting place?"

"Gay Paree, naturally?"

"Right. And we know that Tishman was a political person. He would have been a natural, because he was one of the leaders of the Wallace-for-President movement at Penn State."

"Wasn't he a vice-president who was thought to be a socialist or something?"

"Yep, and some veteran's group was up in arms about the college group marching for what they called a pinko. So he may have been easy-pickings for the recruiters."

"Wait, on this subject a bit longer. My talking with Dusplatov didn't produce a statement of any worth, to be sure, but I did sense, by his manner and the words he used, that he was telling me something. I discussed the meeting with Fooey, and by this time we'd had a chance to read the book and go over it very well and Fooey had an important find. Tell them, Foo."

"In reading the book, and knowing that Dusplatov would not reveal anything like names about the Nevada project, I realized that, in the book, whenever he mentions names or reveals identities of groups, that those persons have died, or they were known to be spies. Either they were caught somehow or by their own admission. There were several instances of Americans or British guys that went to Russia and traded sides. I feel strongly that Dusplatov never once mentioned anyone that didn't fit the bill I just described. I mean, I think that anyone or any group he doesn't name is still alive and I think he feels duty-bound not to give them up, even though he's a grandstanding old fart!"

"And I think, because of the way he told me that he couldn't tell me anything, Fooey is absolutely correct."

"Ah, so 'Paris' could be someone still alive today?"

"Absolutely!"

"Oz and I have another point to make about the spy book and the Venona documents. The book, in more than one place indicates that in most cases, all projects of espionage was supervised by someone in the field. These were 'controls'. We had Adam ask the old man about this and he skirts the issue by saying something like, 'well there could have been one person or there could have been ten'. One very significant thing, we think, appears in both Venona and the book. The book says that one of the messages to Nevada was something like, 'Bring Helen home . . .', but the Venona thing has direct translations of all transcriptions."

"What did you find there?"

"The actual communication was, 'Order the Trojan Prince to bring the Queen of Sparta home . . .' Fooey, you're smiling."

"Sure I am. Paris is the Trojan Prince and Helen was the Spartan Queen. That's obvious, but that's not the real juice in this communication. If the wire was to go to Paris directly it would have been, like, 'Bring Helen home', not, 'Order him to bring her home'. The wire went to someone who was told to order Paris to bring her home. There had to be at least one other person besides Paris involved in this. It probably was a 'control', 'cause who else could order Paris to do something."

"Absolutely! That's exactly what Max and I surmised. Young lady, It's obvious that great minds work in the same way, right?"

"Guys, the work you've done on this is really great."

"Thanks. Max and I had several thoughts about the Mitchell fellow, also."

"And so do I, Oz.'"

"You first, Frank.

"I had asked Chapman to do a background check on Mitchell and there were several things of importance. We know that he was a pre-World War II enlistee. After boot camp he was drafted into the OSS during the war."

"OSS! Wasn't that the precursor of the CIA?"

"Yes."

"And how come that never surfaced during the Nevada investigation?"

"I asked Chapman the same question and he said that in those days they did three levels of investigation relative to time and depth demands. They did what he called a '2-D' search and missed the OSS info."

"That may have made some difference back then."

"I know. When his OSS days were over, and since the Navy lent him to the OSS, he was returned to duty in California after he had his leg broken during a parachute drop near the end of the war."

"Max and I have something else to report. Maxie, tell hem who we saw in Maryland."

"Sure, part of what Chapman sent us through Frank includes military service records. In there I find a copy of Mitchell's enlistment papers and find out that he lived on Kent Island, in Maryland, with his sister. His mother was in a state run nursing home with severe and complicated medical problems. He gets in trouble with the police by stealing a car. A judge gives him the choice to join the military or get sent to reform school. He chose the service, but he was a minor and had to get his sister to sign him in."

"Max, get to the meat of it, already."

"Okay, sure. We went to see the sister in a home down there. The long and short of it is that Dutch, sometime after he gets into the service, has his mom transferred to a swanky private home connected to Johns Hopkins, buys his sister a local bar and restaurant, pays all of the bills probably laundering the money through the bar. Oz and I figured that he kept this up for about twenty years and must have spent around two million bucks. Now where in the hell does a guy like that get that kind of dough?"

" Holy hell, that's fantastic!"

"Listen, folks, there's more. Oz is being kind to include

me in everything, but he's the one with the computer expertise. Show them, Oz."

"Thanks, Max, your humility is heart warming. Anyway, I had mentioned to Adam that we thought it had been a mistake not to have followed up on seeing this Mitchell guy. Anyway, we have about fifteen still shots from the FBI files. They're old, black and white surveillance pictures taken of the suspected contact site in a store in Las Vegas."

"Where did they come from?

"Don't ask! I put them through my computer animation program. I have it on disc here and I showed it to Max. The man's face wasn't clear in the shots, but the one thing we could see clearly was that the man had a limp."

"Holy hell, are you kidding?"

"Fooey, put that disc in your computer and let's take a look."

They all gathered around the computer on the desk in the room off the bedroom, Fooey's office. They watched the loop three times until Fooey hit the stop key and extracted the disc. They returned to the kitchen, amazed at what they had seen.

"My God! Mitchell had a limp. We were told it was more noticeable when he was tired. Spearson had mentioned that he tried to hide it so he could do his time to retirement."

"Well, this is all the more reason to see him."

"Adam, I want to see this man, too."

"That's OK by me, Foo. Is that all right with you, Oz?"

"Max and I will go, as I mentioned before. One other thing as a reminder. If Harry was killed and put in the drone to cover up the evidence, then Mitchell was the last person on earth to see him and maybe put him in that drone!"

The meeting ended after they finished the discussion over more coffee. It had been decided that even though no definitive facts were present, it was very likely that one or more persons, other than Harry, had stolen the device plans and perhaps some log books of Harry's and, perhaps, did away with Harry to keep him quiet and to cast suspicion his way. They were all very anxious to see what Mitchell had to say.

*FEBRUARY 25, 1993: UNITED FLIGHT 1324,*

*FINAL APPROACH, LAX*

Adam and Fooey held hands as the large plane descended slowly towards the Los Angeles airport. Max and Oz were across the aisle from them and they both smiled at the couple. Max sighed and turned to his friend.

"It's good that Frank got the whereabouts of Mitchell. With the information he got, if it had taken longer to find him he may have been dead by the time we got to him."

"Well, we'll hope he's in good enough condition to talk to us. Anyway, this trip gives me a chance to visit with my daughter and the grandkids in Westlake Village. You'll have fun with us for a few days."

The landing was uneventful and after what seemed like a forever wait for the luggage, Oz, Max and Fooey found Adam, who had gone ahead to collect the rental car. It was lunchtime and they decided to use Sepulveda Boulevard, south toward Long Beach and the VA hospital there. With a quick stop in Manhattan Beach for some sandwiches and soft drinks, the trip didn't take very long. Adam and Fooey were scheduled to take the 'red-eye' back east that night; Max and Oz would drop them back at the airport after they saw Mitchell.

As they entered the hospital, all four of them were anxious and it showed. Fooey nervously bit her bottom lip; Adam was chewing gum, which he rarely did. He chomped very quickly like a batter at the plate hoping for a grand slam. Max was humming something and Oz was pumping his arms as they all walked down a long hallway to Mitchell's room. They had been told that they could stay for one hour and they were not to have him talk a great deal.

Entering the room, they were confronted with a thin,

wizened, very ill man. A single sheet covered him and one could see that Mitchell was wasting away. An IV tube was in his arm and an oxygen tube was clipped to the underside of his nose. A pacemaker and monitor stood beside the bed with wires and electrodes snaking under the sheet. He was tilted up slightly and seemed to be staring at the wall-mounted TV, but there was no sound on. Adam stood close to the bed.

"Mr. Mitchell, I'm Adam Kirkendahl and these are friends of mine. I'm the son of Harry Connors. I'm the one that left you a message at your trailer a while back. I also left you messages at the trailer park office. You never bothered to return my calls."

"I know who you are—what the hell are you doing here?"

"You were there when my father disappeared, you worked with him, you were one of the last people to see him on the day of the blast."

"So, what the hell do you want from me?"

"I'll spare you all the details. You're familiar with most of them anyway. The investigation back in '53 concluded that my father was guilty of taking classified documents, basically because he disappeared and couldn't defend himself. My mother has had to live with that fact all these years."

"I'm really touched. Why don't you get me some tissues there on my table and then get the hell out of here!"

Adam's hands were tight fists and his face was getting red. Oz stepped closer to the bed and raised his voice.

"Listen, you son-of-a-bitch, this man has been through a lot trying to track down what happened to his dad. You don't want to talk? Well, don't. You listen for a minute, then. My friend Max, here, and I went to college with Harry. We and this nice young lady have been helping Adam. We positively feel that Harry was not the culprit back in Nevada. He was the victim. We think that he had information that frightened someone and that he was killed. Oh, now you're paying a bit more attention are you? Here's more. 'Paris' and 'Helen'. I bet you haven't heard those names in a long while, have you? You know, your eyes just got a little wider, Mitchell. Are we touching a nerve? What we, and someone in the FBI think is that poor Harry was killed and disposed of in the drone and then the drone was destroyed, on purpose, to cover up the murder and theft of the plans for a secret device."

Mitchell attempted to respond, but he coughed and coughed more heavily. They could see he was having trouble catching his breath. After a moment, he looked at them all bleary-eyed and gasping.

"I could care less what the shit you all think. You're talking about forty-year-old crap. Get the hell out and don't come back."

"No, we're not going anywhere. I'm telling you what we think. We know that Tishman called Harry early that morning about some problems and Harry drove to the airbase. You knew he was sniffing around about some bad radiation data and you and maybe others probably had orders to steal the trigger-device documents. When you saw Harry, you figured you could kill two birds with one stone. Steal the documents, kill Harry and lay the blame on him. According to the briefing notes we saw, you were the last one to be at the drone. In your rush, you neglected to plug in one of the cables to the dummy and that's why Tishman got a bad reading that morning. You had to be sure that the drone was destroyed, but that was easy since you were in charge of the instrumentation.

An interview with one of the technicians reveals that you sent him out of the operations van for a smoke. Convenient for you to do what you had to do, right Dutch? You just fiddled with the dials so the drone would be close enough to the detonation to be destroyed. You also put a torn piece of the cover page from the stolen documents in Harry's car. No one locked his car in those days. My pal and I, here, visited a nice lady in Maryland named Isabel Garmish recently. Sound familiar, Dutch? How in the hell could you afford to keep your mother so well and for so long? You sure as hell never won a lottery. Or maybe you did. Was it a Russian lottery?"

Mitchell held his chest and coughed like he was going to die. Finally his hacking eased off.

"What bullshit! You give me a laugh, you all do. I'm here with emphysema and liver cancer. I got water on my heart and they got me hooked up to some electric crap to keep my heart going. And here you bastards are. What are you trying to do, scare me? Or maybe you'll turn me in and than what? You going to kill me? Shit! I'm three-quarters there already."

"No, we can't scare you, but we're staying here until you talk to us, Mitchell. There's more. We know you were in the OSS. We know you killed for them Mr. Paris!

"I don't know what the hell you're talking about. Paris, Helen, and why not Kukla, Fran and Ollie, for Christ's sake?"

"I said we're staying until you talk to us, Mitchell."

"OK, then. I remember Harry. A very nice guy, a goody two-shoes, salt of the earth; and his wife was cute, too. I'm watching a football game here and you all won't leave unless I talk? OK, here it is, is this what you want to hear? I was with freakin' Helen and Paris. We took off and Harry was put in the drone and poof! Is that what you want to hear? Now fuck the hell off and leave me the hell alone."

"Why, you bastard, I should kill you!"

"No, Adam, please."

"Calm down, Adam. She's right."

"OK, OK, Max, he's not worth the trouble. He'll be in hell soon enough. We're leaving."

"You two wait outside for Max and me."

Fooey and Adam walked into the hallway. She was trembling and Adam, head down, was seething.

"With all the information we have, assumptions, facts and all. And now, after seeing him, I guess we're finished with all this."

"And you're comfortable with our conclusions? I mean, really, can you be at ease and put this behind us? Do you think you can be truly finished with this? And can we tell your mom that it's over?"

"Yep! Yes, Fooey, I can . . . and we will tell mom."

Max and Oz stared at Mitchell looking at the silent TV.

"So, my young friend says that you're not worth killing. You are a bastard, Mitchell. Max, would you have any problem with me pulling this 'cocker's' plug?"

"Nope. No problem at all."

After a few seconds, they turned on their heels and walked out of the room and into the long hallway.

# EPILOG

He sat on the roof deck of the white stucco building he owned, smoking his afternoon Havana. He had been fishing that morning and his catch was being prepared by one of the three women in his employ. For supper that night he would have his favorite meal, quenelles in shrimp soup.

The sun made the sea a field of shimmering mercury as he looked to the south toward Sardinia. He smiled and thought that he had had a marvelous life. He'd be damned if he had wanted to work all his life and he'd be damned if he was going to help them blow up the world and radiate themselves into oblivion. He exhaled, and the cloud of cigar smoke disappeared over the Tyrrhenian Sea.